From Porn to Poetry 2

Clean Sheets Celebrates the Erotic Mind

Edited by
Susannah Indigo and Brian Peters

Samba Mountain Press
Colorado
2003

Samba Mountain Press
P.O. Box 4741
Englewood, CO 80155
www.sambamountain.com

ISBN 0-971-66234-7

FIRST EDITION: MAY 2003

Printed in the United States of America

Cover photograph of Jane Duvall © Jim Duvall
Cover design by J.J. Designs

Contents

Fiction

Essays

Poetry

Introduction

Clean Sheets Magazine delights in its contribution to the tapestry of quality writing on the Web. Each week we weave still more funny, loving, literate, erotic thoughts for an international audience who make it worth all the hard work. This book represents a broad overview of what we love best from the weekly Web magazine, along with brand new stories from some of our favorite writers. We are thrilled to bring you this second book in the *From Porn to Poetry* series, in part because we still find it rather amazing to see all this talent in one place, in print, and to revel in the heat and the sheer diversity of the writing.

The magazine relies on a huge amount of generosity to make publication possible, from our beloved contributors, to our extraordinary staff, to our friends at Toys in Babeland. This book would not be possible without all of them. Nor would it be possible without the dedicated efforts of Nola Summers, who, among other things, proofread every word.

We hope that you love reading the book as much as we loved putting it together—thanks for your support, and we hope to see you again this week on the Web!

Susannah Indigo and Brian Peters
May 2003

From Porn to Poetry 2

Clean Sheets Celebrates the Erotic Mind

The Lucky Dick Club

Diane Fisher

The night after I won the lottery I made a list of all the men I'd ever slept with. I'm not one of those girls who pretends she can't remember. There's only been a couple dozen, and I can recall every moment that my skin has been stroked, every time another human being has spent their energy on pleasing me, no matter what their real intentions might have been. This is something basic that men would be wise to tattoo on their hearts—*women remember.* We believe that it all matters, even when we're drinking and dancing at the clubs and acting like post-second-wave-feminist-entrepreneurial-sex-goddesses with tattoos on our breasts and condoms tucked inside our stockings. *We remember. Girls want dreams to come true.*

Money's never been much in my dreams, though, so it's ironic I would win so much. Pay off my bills, buy a new car, share with friends, family long gone—then what? I have what I need, I don't have kids, I live my days peering at the world through the vision of things sexual, hiding in my imagination more often than not, consumed by music and art and passion and ideas. I think of the French film *Amelie* and it comes to me, the need for whimsy and kindness and appreciation of some of the great lovers I've known.

I count them. I rate them. I am surprised to find that for every two bad lovers there is at least one great one to offset them. There are men whose passion still leaves imprints on my skin, there are men whose every word of affection was like diamonds and rubies and pearls falling from their tongues, enriching my soul with the bright colors of the morning sun. I check off the bad lovers, laughing, hoping for them that somewhere along the line they've learned to pay attention, learned that they need to do something in this world beside just take up space and waste the time of girls who matter.

Michael J., New York City—he's first on the list that remains. I want to share my lotto winnings with him, and the others on the list, and I want them to know it's because they were great lovers, but I never want them to know it's from Emily, this girl who now lives in London and who will never forget. I ask my lawyer, Jackson—who happens to also be the man I'm currently sleeping with—how to do this, and we begin.

It's a simple letter. We copy the MacArthur *Genius Grant* idea, the people who call up scientists and artists and philosophers out of the blue—surprise!—and tell them they've won a fortune for their good work. Only mine's a bit more personal. We start calling it *The Lucky Dick Club* privately, but give it a more formal name for legal purposes.

To: Michael J.
From: **THE LDC FOUNDATION**

You have been selected by our committee to receive an *LDC Powerballs Grant*. Our selection is done in secret, and there are no strings attached to this award. The first of four checks for $25,000 is enclosed; additional checks will be issued on the first of September in the next three years, for a total of $100,000.

You are considered a pioneer in touch, a kind and passionate man in a world of sloppiness and unreturned calls. You have demonstrated particular strength and insights with women. LDC grant recipients are singled out annually by the foundation for extraordinary creativity in their desires. You have been rated as a bold, experimental lover, whose social and philosophical themes speak to the heart of modern society. You have shown a marked capacity for self-direction, and a respect and passion for the female gender that should be emulated by all mankind.

We share with you one of our committee member's recommendations:

I remember Michael J. . . . he was tall and kind and had eyes a girl could get lost in. He took the trouble to be romantic—there were strawberries and peonies and cream for tea—and he took the time to worship my body from head to toe with his kisses and his compliments. I am sure he knew prettier women; I am sure he had way more experience than me; but when I was with him I knew that I was the most sensual woman in all of New York City. He had hands that could make love to me all by themselves, hands almost like a masseuse, knowing, caressing, finding the spots that mattered, carrying me up beyond my physical sensations onto a higher plain of loving. When he would finally enter me I knew that there was only one reason that we had such beautiful bodies that fit together like two pieces of a puzzle, and it was so that he could drive me hard and

long into the night until I had not a single ion of negative energy left in my soul, left only with light and enthusiasm and gratitude for existing in such a beautiful fucking world.
The LDC Foundation is proud of your performance, Michael J. Do carry on.

Michael J. is in his forties now, he's a man in New York City, he's not likely to ever remember who it was, since I didn't give any identifying details. We send the letter off. I'm going crazy waiting. Jackson loves me passionately to help ease my anxiety, and I swear he seems to be working on becoming a better lover every single day . . . but I don't even know Michael or any of his friends well enough to check up on what's happening. Finally, three weeks later the check is cashed, and the "foundation" never even receives a call in question. But I'm betting he thinks about it every single time he looks at a woman, and maybe even every time his lucky dick gets hard.

The second grant goes to a lover from almost fifteen years ago. *I remember Allen McD, now in Toronto . . . he is the hottest man I've ever known, hot in that way that you can't even describe to friends until they've experienced something like it. He'd back me into a corner in a club or the subway or just a doorway on the street and begin to make love to me. He made me feel like I was born to fuck. It wasn't really a sensual thing, more like two animals in the night in heat and in need. It wasn't a grab and grope thing like guys do, the way women hate, this was in the words and the look and the need to be*

4

inside of me, the need expressed as though I was a drug that he would die if he didn't get another hit of immediately. I began to walk differently during and after Allen McD., a little more swing to my hips, a lot more confidence, an unwritten sign across my chest that said "I am hotter than thou." Allen McD. wrote those words across me, and I know he wrote them on other women, and whether it was all because we had raging hormones or were nymphos for a while or because he was a troubled soul in so many other ways, it doesn't matter, because it stays with me today and I still can exude the same air to any man I want every single time I walk down the street.

The check is cashed, again a month later. Do they sit and ponder, do they hide it, do they think it's a joke, or finally deposit the check just to see? This time I still have a former business acquaintance in common who works with Allen McD. I wait another month and call her up on some business pretense and chat about things, and then casually ask what good old Allen's up to these days. "He seems *really* happy," she says. "He got engaged last month . . . and he's taking her on a long honeymoon to the Grand Caymans . . . you know, he laughs a lot, more than he used to. He ought to bottle it and sell it, whatever it is he's got going on these days."

I'm inspired.

I've finally worked my way up to the man who broke my heart, the lover I had to debate about when making the list. He gave me everything, but then he took it away. Still, time alters perception, and what I remember most about him today is the loving. *I remember Nick B., Boston . . . he came to me one day like a bolt of lightning. He tied me up—it's what I do with all the girls, he told me, it's what turns me on—he taught me to love the feel of hemp rope against my bare skin, he showed me a different kind of dance, he could control my every move,*

5

and he could change the way I breathe. The fact that he did this with way more than one woman at a time more often than not was disappointing, but doesn't change those midnight hours when I was wrapped up by him and permanently marked with his brand of love.

I still know Nick B., in that awful ex-lover/friend/acquaintance way, when you don't really know a damned thing about each other anymore but pretend that it still matters that you chat occasionally when you're in town. So I wait, and I call him three months after the check is cashed. He's doing great, he tells me, he's finally finished his novel, he has a new inspired state. I ask him if he's in love, after telling him about my new love, Jackson. "No," he says, "I decided about three months ago to become celibate for a year and to really think about my history, and what it is that I need to be doing . . . why are you calling me, by the way, what's up?" I tell him I do volunteer work for a non-profit business now, and just need a stateside referral in Boston from him.

He laughs. "You were always a do-gooder, Emily."

And then it occurs to me, he has *no idea* how much good I can do. There is more to this story. I am thinking too small, too personally, focused only on my own memories. There are a million lovers out there and more than half of them are bad. I'm watching Jackson sneak in books like *From Porn to Poetry, Herotica, 1000 Ways to Tongue Your Lover,* and God knows he gets sexier all the time even when I think he can't get any better, but those books aren't being read by lousy lovers. This will never do. Jackson often says in his lawyerly way that "money changes everything," and maybe he's right.

I can change the world. *Fuck locally, award globally.* Life is short. Towers fall down, young people die, still, rudeness is everywhere and lovers continue to thought-lessly cause pain.

I can change this.

This is my calling in life, to rid the world of bad lovers. There are *so* many women I know, and they'll share. *They remember.* We can expand; we can raise funds; we can sneak it to the press; we can inspire lovers everywhere, and the question on everyone's mind will be—what would someone remember about *me?* If I work at this long and hard and cleverly enough, by the time we get to post-third-or-fourth-wave-feminist-entrepreneurial-sex-goddess girls who will still probably have tattoos on their breasts and condoms tucked inside their stockings, *they will remember differently, and perhaps all of their dreams will come true.*

Jumping Jacks

Debbie Ann

We go to a playparty, in a space we've been to many times before. I take off all my clothes, just like I usually do, and we go downstairs.

Okay, he says, *do ten jumping jacks.*

And I can't, won't, don't. He sits in a chair, looks at me and says, *I'm waiting.*

I squirm. I want to please. I want to obey and I can't do this, don't make me do this, I'll feel so stupid. Nobody else is doing jumping jacks. Nobody else ever does jumping jacks here. My breasts will bounce, people will look at me. I can't.

And he's still waiting. *After your jumping jacks, you'll get a spanking, but until you do them, I'm just going to sit here.*

I try kneeling and begging and pleading. He pushes me away.

Go on. Stand up. You can't even do this simple thing? I'm going to make you do push ups next.

No . . . no . . . no. I can't. I squirm. It's still early, but people are here and the space we're in is pretty visible. I'm miserable. I can't disobey so much as to actually walk away, but I can't do that either. I feel stuck and trapped and unhappy. I want out. I don't want to be seen or watched. I don't want to see anyone else. I want the ground to open up and swallow me whole. I think I'd rather die, but I know that's not true. I could never do gym stuff—couldn't kick balls, or catch them, or hit them. I hated gym.

I feel so uncoordinated.

I'll look so stupid. I struggle with that. Why do I care? But it's not just that—I'll look stupid to other people, but I'll look awful and dumb in front of him too, but why should that matter? But it does, and maybe it is the other people, too, and how out of place it'll look, and they can all do this and I can't. I stand there, but my own internal anxiety over it won't allow me to stand still for long.

I'd rather be cut, pierced, whipped, tortured, flogged. I can do any of that, and I can't do this simple stupid thing. I'm terrified out of my mind. The more time that goes by, the worse it gets. It's my own fear—and my own mind preventing me—I hate fighting myself.

I think about it. It makes me cry. Kids making fun of me in school, people choosing sides and not being chosen. It's everything that hurt.

I stare. I stomp my feet. I pout.

I hate this.

I don't know how to find a way through it. It should be the simplest thing in the world but it's not, it's everything, it's my father making me exercise.

I can't. It takes too much coordination. I can't do it. It's not possible. I put my hands over my eyes, stuff my fingers in my mouth, and feel like I've never had to do anything harder in my whole life.

I can't tell if five hours or twenty minutes have gone by. We seem to exist in this bubble, the party a blur around us. I can't see or hear or focus. I want out. I briefly think, well, I could just safeword. Not that we've even remotely negotiated a safeword. Right. But I can't. Now

I know I'll be miserable if I do this, but more miserable if I don't. If all the rest was uphill, this is the top of the hill. It is a matter of pride. It is such a stupid little thing and that only makes it worse—'tis noble, perhaps, to agonize over a branding, a cutting, a whipping, but jumping fucking jacks? Right.

I try bargaining. I try denial. I try any of the other stages of grief that I can remember.

It's wearing us both out. Well, more accurately, it's wearing me out. I'm emotionally and physically exhausted from anger to crying to pleading to trying to disappear. The other people in the room have stopped mattering to me. This is personal. This is just between us. This is mine to get through. Nobody else really exists.

. . . and then I do them. In a haze . . . and then just crumple into a heap and cry.

And he walks over to me, gently puts me face down, rearranges my limbs, which are completely limp, and sits on my back and starts to spank me, and I sob harder and then softer, sniffling, ragged breathing, and I know I'm safe and cared for and not stupid and awful and it's going to be okay. And I love being spanked like nothing else, it's the sweetest reward in the world, it's the only thing that makes me feel loved and cherished.

And when the spanking is over, I curl up under a blanket and fall into a half sleep of emotional exhaustion. I made it through this. It wouldn't make sense to anyone in the world but me/us—it was just my own personal terror, dredged up into the open, and it can't ever be so terrifying again. It can only ever be the second time.

Sheet Lightning

Rebecca Lu Kiernan

Grinning blonde weatherman in a stone gray flannel suit,
Neon cobalt eyes, wire frame glasses, eye-popping red tie,
Licking my lips I think, "I'd fuck you blind."
I shock myself at this pathetic hunger for a stranger.
But how much more intense was my knowledge of the
Whimsical one who slept beside me in the almond rice
Bed and T-shirt sheets whispering unbearable pleasures
Wetly against my neck, groping me inside him, writhing
At the whip, breathlessly whispering, "Come for me."
Pinching, trembling, crushing
Clawing at my soul, crying out my name in shameless
Ecstasy, baptizing me with sweat, saliva, tears,
Charging relentlessly with every intention of turning me
Inside-out.
Seventy-five percent chance of sheet lightning,
Uncalculable risk of actual strike.
So much hinges on geography.

Troy

Julia Peters

Troy rises, like a specter, out of my bed. It's Saturday evening and we've been here since Friday. I'm at the end of my rope but, somehow, can't let go.

"Troy," I say, "I'm exhausted."

"Then let me do the work."

The sun is going down again. The same old shadows stretch across the ceiling in a familiar embrace. My windows are cracked open and the deepening cool air curls in with the smell of tobacco as my neighbors smoke on the stoop. He runs his hands along my calves, massaging twenty-four hours of soreness out of them. Bending down, he brings his head to where his hands are. I can see the muscles in his back unfold and tense beneath the skin. His legs are stretched out behind him, dangling off the bed, beautiful and undignified. His brown, curly hair laps at my thighs and I'm waiting, hoping that his mouth will follow suit.

"That feels so good," I say, inanely. There's no way to tell him all of it; that he's bringing my calves to life, making them more than merely functional. He makes me feel the smoothness of my own skin. He makes me raise my hips up. I ask for things and know I can get them.

"That feels so good," I say again and he rubs his

cheek along the inside of my right leg, mirroring the touch with his palm on my other leg. Long, taut minutes go by and then Troy is there, spreading me open and putting his mouth on me yet again. And it's just as exciting as the first time, all wet shock and comfort.

"Troy," I say, but he doesn't acknowledge me, except to kiss my whole pussy in one strong, open-mouthed suck. I say his name again and again, half to myself, and run my hands over his shoulders and into his hair. These gestures are routine. They're what I've done with every man I've been with. It's as if I can't give as good as I get. He slowly works a finger inside me, crooking it upward and gripping me with his palm while he kisses my clit. I roll lazily beneath him, too tired to moan, and just sigh as he pulls another dazzling orgasm from my body and I shimmer in the new darkness of my bedroom.

It's been a month of this, almost from the beginning. We met in the kitchen at a party, hiding out from love we didn't want. Troy was avoiding an ex-girlfriend; I was waiting out friends who were insisting on setting me up with someone. We sipped our free beers the same way, as if punctuating run-on arguments we were having in our heads. He caught that, smiled and pointed it out. I was caught by his smirk above the green bottle, his soft voice. I felt my pupils flare up involuntarily, spotting my target, knowing in that moment that I could have him and that I might want to. We introduced ourselves.

"As in Helen of?" He shook his head before I even finished the question.

"You get that a lot, huh?" I asked, leaning on the kitchen sink next to him.

"I get that a bit," he said. "My older sister is Teresa, so I guess my parents had a 'T' thing. But it comes with a lot of preconceptions."

"Hmm. I always thought it would be a beautiful nickname to be called."

"Why's that?" He smiled warily.

"Well, because of the preconceptions. I guess you've heard them. Helen of Troy. Most beautiful woman in the world. Everyone wants to feel that way to somebody. And also, for a woman to be called Troy, that would be kind of tough and butch, which is cool. I don't know. Beauty and destruction in one package you couldn't live without. Sounds like a love affair."

He looked at me for a long moment and then extended his hand. "What's your name again?" he said. I told him, and found him just like that, because I wasn't looking for anyone. How it always goes. A few days later we slept together. Also how it always goes. Then it went differently.

"Kate," Troy says into my answering machine. I'm in the middle of lining my eyes and didn't even try to answer the phone. My heart jumps, at once thrilled and guilty, because I want to hear his voice. It's been a week since our marathon, and I've only seen him once. I miss him, and our schedules are all off. But I'm getting ready for a second date with someone else.

"I'd tell you to kiss me, Kate, but that's a little obvious. Fuck me, Kate, is funny but vulgar. So Kate. Um. Love me, Kate. Now's the part where I hang up in embarrassment. Ha. Okay. Call me. Bye."

The eyeliner has rolled off my dresser and onto the floor. I stare at myself in the mirror, all made up. His voice. His awkwardness. The show tune reference and the sweetness. This man has me pinned to the spot. After about a minute, I put on my lipstick with a slow, shaking hand. I play the tape so the message won't be waiting when I get back and then head out to meet someone whose last name I keep getting wrong.

The doorbell rings the next day, cutting through my Saturday afternoon, my pleasant aloneness. I'm at home forcing myself to read up on troubleshooting Java for my job.

"Yes?" I ask the buzzer.

"Me," says Troy.

He comes up the stairs, bass guitar banging against the banister. He's on his way to band practice, where he's often going to or coming from.

"Hey, me," I say.

"Hey, you," he replies and kisses me simply on the lips. Then again on my forehead. "I brought a gift."

"Oh," I say, nervous and pleased.

He pulls out a somewhat ratty record of, of course, *Kiss Me Kate.*

"Original cast recording," he says brightly. "Thrift store. Did you get my message?"

"Yes," I say. This is the part where I'm supposed to say something. The easiest way to cover would be to take him to bed. But my pillows smell like second date man, who left here at 2 a.m. after I realized, and told him, that I'm not really single. Something I haven't told Troy, that I'm with him.

"So I know it's unexpected. And actually, I have to get to rehearsal. But I have time to kiss you."

"I have time to kiss you back," I say. We stand braced in the doorway, the bass and my textbook and the album forgotten on the floor. We kiss the same kiss again and again. What wasn't there with second date man, what hasn't been in my life for years and years, is there now, in the remolding and perfecting of this kiss. There's so much I want to give him, but I'm unprepared.

"Can I kiss you everywhere?" I ask him.

"Yes," he whispers, against his better judgment and

time constraints.

"With everything?"

"Kate—"

"You have to go," I say. "It's okay."

"Not yet." We push the door shut together and I lead him into the living room. He sits on the couch and I make a comical leap on top of him. He slides out of his shirt while I work on his pants and mine. His body. My God. I'm at his broad feet, licking my way up to the dimple of his right knee as he lies lengthwise on the couch. Still kissing, I work my way up from crouched to spread over him like a blanket of limbs. We lie and kiss in this fierce press, grinding against each other, until he pushes me back and sits up, pulls me to him. My legs are around him. He paws beneath my T-shirt with one hand and through the pockets of his jeans on the floor with the other, producing the condom.

"Boy Scout," I moan as I free his cock from his boxers.

"Always prepared," he says, rolling the condom on. He gets inside me and we move on each other, hard and laughing.

"Kisses for Kate," he says, kissing my neck and shoulders in time with our thrusts. He doesn't say the other thing, because I haven't said it yet. He came here to take me and I won't let him. Instead, I bounce in his lap and claw at his back. I start to move toward my orgasm, wanting to keep moving how he likes, but it's so hard and my clit is so tight. I come down for him in shallow movements with shallow breath.

"Come, honey, come on," he says and I do, full of him. I change it and move how I like, deep rotations, as he burrows into me, as my rhythm makes him come. He yells out, his head thrown back, somewhere between a laugh and a sob. He never muffles it or screams into my shoulder. It's right out there and I watch it with as much excitement as I feel it, his come kissing me back between my legs.

We make real plans a few days later, and I meet Troy for a movie with a head full of doubt. The conversation won't work. We're talking about the book the movie was based on, but I didn't read it, so I don't agree with his argument against the movie. We're walking with no aim and I ask if we should go to his house and make dinner. He agrees. The minute we get inside, I give him a kiss to make sure things are all right, then try to kiss the disagreement away. We're standing in the hallway, and his shirt is off quick as a candy wrapper. I'm kissing him thoughtlessly and well, move down to his chest. He pushes his erection forward to meet my belly. He pants hard and undoes my blouse.

"I want you right here," I say. He says nothing. I keep kissing and it feels strange, like it's something he's allowing me to do. His palms sit on my hips.

"What?" I peer into his face with a raised eyebrow.

"Nothing."

"What, Troy?"

"We were in the middle of a conversation."

"I thought I was continuing the conversation."

"By fucking me in the hallway."

I let go of him, step away from his arousal and anger. "Okay. You can come over unannounced and fuck me, but I can't do the same. Thanks."

"That's not it. I'm sorry to stop this cold, but—"

"What? I want you, all right? Why is that a problem?" Paris wanted Helen and accepted the consequences. The most romantic story there is. Or maybe he was an asshole. She ended up with her husband anyway, after all that war and death. Stupidly, I babble some of this at him and make no sense.

"Jesus, Kate. I'm not a myth. And I'm sorry, but I didn't like that movie. Why is that a problem?"

I can't see how I look, but I know I'd hate it. Rejected in his hallway, my blouse unbuttoned and no shoes on. For a moment I push the scene further on to what could have happened: my leg braced against the wall, Troy pushing inside of me as we clutch each other's hands. What I can't explain to him is that I wanted to give it to him as a present. He told me once that he'd never made love standing up, and he fantasizes about it. We're close in height so it could work. I loved the record album. I love how he makes me feel. I love to watch how he moves through the world. I even love fighting with him, but I want to apologize, to give him something he'll love. But I'm unprepared.

"I'm sorry," I say. Because I can't explain it well enough to make it work. I turn my back and button up my shirt because I don't want him to see.

"Are you cold?"

"A little. I need a sweater." I stand there and stare at him like maybe he'll knit me one. He looks down at his feet. I realize what he must think, that I just want to screw him rather than deal with the fight. He doesn't offer me anything.

"Can I borrow a sweater?" I say softly.

"Yeah," he says. "Take what you need." Then he goes down to hall to the kitchen, to fix me a silent dinner.

The next day I take the train home from work, thinking, *why learn new computer languages when I'm so inept at English?* It's the worst weather we've had in weeks, the worst since I've met Troy. Winter will not come quietly this year; it's rampaging and screaming already and it's only October. I think of his day job, booking tours for bands that are just barely of interest to the college crowd. Not what he was looking for, but it's working out and he can be around people who love music, keep up with the industry, be with his band. He picked the right thing and it's an impressive choice. I miss my stop and stay onboard until I get to his.

Walking uptown, I recognize the markers of a night at Troy's—the bodega where we buy condoms and ice cream, the statue of the Blessed Virgin in the playing field of a Catholic school. A pay phone. For five minutes, I face off against it in the rain. My thoughts read, *call him, don't call him, love him, don't love him.* Why love wins is hard to say. Maybe because it already did, maybe because I think I might be too late. My quarters roll in to the slot and I wait, every pulse in my body stopping between rings. He picks up.

"Hello?"

"It's raining," I say.

"I can see that. You left your umbrella at work, didn't you?"

"Yes. I love you."

"What?"

"I'm two blocks from your house. And I swear to God, Troy, we can talk about it until it's time to go to work tomorrow. I should have told you before. But I just want to be with you right now. That's what it's always been for me, when we're together. Because I love you."

There's silence. I picture his hand gliding up and down the phone cord in thought. He does that sometimes with the mike stand when he sings backup. I saw it when his band played a local club last month. It made me think of other things.

"I'll dry you off," he says, and I practically throw the phone into the receiver. On the dash to his apartment, I hit every puddle I can.

Troy is spread out beneath me, the bedsheets curled

in a heap around him like a frame around a perfect photograph. The sheets were unmade when I got here and we're just going to keep unmaking them. Everything is damp and warm, from my boots drying by the radiator to his shoulders which got covered with my wet hair. I'm over him and I look down the length of my torso to take in all of our nakedness. My hips bloom out around him, so much rounder, and I echo this roundness with my movement, circling slowly like a belly dancer. I clutch at him sweetly with the muscles inside and a moan slides from between his lips. He reaches up to hold my breasts, rolling my nipples between his fingers, smoothing the rain off. I take his hands and bring them to my mouth.

"Just for you, now," I say, rising high, coming down around him. "All for you." His fingers part my lips and I suckle at them, hungry for his taste and his reaction. I ride his cock, deliberately slow so as to stretch out our joy. We chose each other with little thought and now I've stolen him, running off without a word of sense. The thing that always got me about Paris and Helen, maybe any story, is that they somehow know after one look. That could be simple lust, or a dramatic device, but it happens so rarely. All I can do now is try to do it well, and take turns with Troy, being lover and beloved.

God of Fuck

Isabelle Carruthers

The editor's life: this is the final manuscript of the night, one of a large stack of fiction submissions I've taken to bed to read. The last, and by far the worst. Adam is stretched out beside me, quietly reading his weekly dissident rag. For the past two hours, he's endured my inane commentary, sighs of appreciation and snorts of disbelief, his only reaction an occasional sidelong glance of amusement or, less frequently, a peek over my shoulder to read for himself. But now, as I toss the pages aside with a groan, he lowers his magazine to make room for conversation.

"That bad, huh?"

"It isn't even a story, just a fuck scene. *Big Throbbing Cock* and *Tight Juicy Pussy*, nothing inventive. And *Oh God!* this and *Oh God!* that, over and over. I finally had to count them, because I couldn't believe anyone could write such lousy dialogue. *Oh God!*, eleven times. No one says *Oh God!* that much when they're fucking, unless they suffer a deplorable lack of imagination."

With a dramatic sigh, I shove the litter of papers off the bed and snuggle under the blankets to wait for him.

He *tsks* in my direction, chiding me for my arrogance. "That's not true. You say it pretty often." He's smiling, playfully, and I'm not sure whether it's a joke or a challenge. But I am sure that he's mistaken, and my mouth gapes in protest as he discards his magazine and turns off the bedside lamp. "I wasn't counting," he adds, sliding beneath the bedcovers to curl his arms around me, "but I'd bet you said *Oh God!* a lot more than eleven times last night."

"I most certainly did not," I retort icily, resisting his embrace. I'm offended at the accusation and, even worse, aghast at the possibility that he might be telling the truth. I'd always imagined myself more eloquent than that, even in the throes of passion.

"Elisabeth, you say *Oh God!* all the time when we're making love," he insists, amused and undaunted by my reaction. "Why not just admit it?"

"Yeah, okay . . . maybe it slips out sometimes, once or twice, in the heat of the moment. But it's just a noise, a sound effect. *Oh God!* Like when you stub your toe or discover you've bounced a check. You make it sound like I'm praying for an orgasm or something," I complain.

"It does seem like a prayer sometimes. Especially when you're on your knees."

"*Pffft,*" I say, missing the point of his humor. "I'm an atheist. I don't do that."

I consider the matter closed, and assume I've made whatever point I intended. Ready to forgive his minor transgression, I shift in bed and begin to move closer, but he's not finished yet. He's still having a laugh, too loudly, at my expense.

"I'm an atheist, too," he reminds me, "but I never say *Oh God!* And, definitely, never during sex."

This may be true, because I don't think I've ever heard him say it. But there's no way I'll admit that now. "Of course you do," I say, frustrated. "Even if you don't realize, it just pops out. The God blurt."

"No, never."

He's too confident, and I'm not. And there's some quirk of my personality that gets the best of me in situations like this. I never know when to shut up, even when I might be wrong.

"Okay, wise ass," I challenge. "So, what do you say when you drop something heavy on your foot?"

He ponders this for only a second, grinning at me. *"Ouch,"* he says, and his hand drifts over my bare thigh, settling comfortably between the argument. I pull my legs together, immobilizing his wrist, but he doesn't seem to notice as he explores whatever he can still reach. One fingertip wiggles free to trace the satin-smooth cleft beneath his hand. I toss him a dirty look and he smiles back, unrepentant.

"You're running late for an appointment and your car has a flat tire."

"'*Shit.*' And I kick the tire, because that's what real men do." His hand is deliberate between my thighs, that roaming finger teasing the lips of my cunt, idly stroking. He finds my clit and taps it gently, as if trying to get my attention. I do my best to ignore him and resume my interrogation with prosecutorial zeal.

"You've overdrawn your checking account."

"Fuck me," he answers, his smile spreading into a sardonic grin.

"Fuck what?" The adventurous finger chooses this moment to penetrate with sudden boldness. I gasp and try to wiggle away. But I don't try very hard.

"Fuck me," he says again, softer than he should, closer than before, and these words linger against my ear in an entirely new context. Soft lips define the curve of my breast, seeming to wander without direction before discovering a peaked nipple with gentle tug of teeth and

tongue. The friction between my legs is no longer aimless, and I forget all about God.

"Fuck me." Now my voice is a whispered echo of his, and the tattered shreds of my argument fall apart along with my thighs. Adam takes advantage of this opening and pushes another finger inside, twisting gently into the moist heat of my body. He quickly finds the single sweet spot that makes me breathless, and his fingers curve inward, pressing rhythmically, insistently. Too soon, my tongue is tipped with the dreaded phrase, and I can't stop it, even when I bite my lip in a vain effort to remain silent.

"Oh God!" I whimper, clutching at his shoulders as I come. And I say it again, and again, and again, help-lessly, *Oh God!* with each burst of pleasure that begins in my cunt and spreads outward, flexing my fingers and toes. And then, just as helplessly, I dissolve in laughter when my mind clears and I realize what I've said.

"Four," he murmurs, and I smile beneath his smiling kiss, chagrined but somehow pleased in spite of my fail-ure.

"Fuck you," I respond, sweetly. My fingers find and encircle the rigid column of his flesh, pulling him closer.

Adam enters me with a muted groan, pushing deep and almost painfully against my womb. His hands slide beneath my hips and lift me to the unrelenting pressure of his cock, holding me so tightly that it's impossible to move except toward him. I strain upward, rocking in a motion that soon becomes uncontrollable, frantic and primitive.

And yes, it is *Big and Throbbing*, this cock that fills me, and my *Pussy is Tight and Juicy* with the madness of wanting, and language fails me again, as it always does when he fucks me. The words form on my lips, unbidden, but I say them willingly now, *Oh God!* breathing it in and

24

crying it out, no longer eloquent but no longer caring. Reduced at last to the worst dialogue imaginable, I hear myself sob and gasp, moaning to the God of Fuck, moaning the syllables of his name, a torrent of sound as desperate and hopeful as any prayer could be.

Much later, when our frenzied coupling has finally given way to languid movements and contented sighs, I see the smile playing on his face. He doesn't have to tell me what he's thinking.

Yes, I did say it more than eleven times.

Maybe even more than fifty.

And my prayer was answered.

Amen.

How To Look At Girls

H.L. Shaw

Ah, girls. Being one myself, I know how easy it is to get annoyed by the stares girls get, but man oh, man, there's nothing better to look at than beautiful women. The trick is, of course, in not getting caught staring.

Two Silhouettes on the Shade

It was only recently that I learned the finer points of girlwatching from a friend of mine. We were at a party, both sighing as a lovely young lady made her way out of the terraces of the garden, her long skirt trailing slightly behind her in the grass. My friend, Allen, murmured something about her legs.

"What about her legs?" I said, "Her skirt hits the ground; they're completely covered."

He nodded towards her. "Look more carefully".

And then I saw it. The sun was behind her, its rays spilling out around her body and making her seem to glow and shimmer. But the long skirt was too thin for such rays, and I could clearly see through that skirt the shape of her calves, her thighs, her . . .

"Oh. My!"

I was transfixed as her shapely legs crossed, opened

and closed as she made her way down towards us. She wasn't wearing any panties, and I could even see that she didn't do much bikini shaving.

Allen nudged me, "Your mouth is open, hon; don't get caught staring like that."

Since this joyous occasion, I've taken a keener interest in the angle of the sun and the thickness of fabrics. Thankfully, most women's clothing is cheaply made, and the skirts are easy enough to look through in a bright light. This angle usually requires that you be a certain distance away, which makes it difficult for the observed to notice just exactly where you're looking.

Twin Peeks

Cleavage is not so easy.

A beautiful friend of mine complained to me recently, "No man has looked into my eyes since I was twelve!" Indeed, this seems to be the area where most men become mesmerized by the mammary, and the downward tilt of the chin and the tops of the eyelids give them away every time.

I'm always impressed when I know a man is looking at my cleavage yet I can't seem to catch him at it. This kind of skill is thrilling, as it lets me know he's sensitive to my privacy, but not insensitive to my charms. If I like him, at some point I'll usually lean over all the way (to pick something up) just to give him a really good view of my "girls." If I'm feeling a little mean, I'll look up and finally catch him looking, giving him a wry smile.

The key to not getting caught is, of course, to not look all the time. There is no good way to disguise a constant stare, and glancing away when you get caught only confirms your guilt. If possible, always get your one good look in right at the beginning, before she has noticed you. Once you're chatting with the woman in question, it's too late for a good long look, so make sure to stand to one side as she approaches, letting your gaze fall across her breasts as you nonchalantly scan the room.

In conversation, observe her eye-contact habits and make a mental note of the rhythm of them. Does she tend to look away when it's her turn to speak? Does she shy away from direct eye contact as you're speaking to her? These sorts of habits often have a delicious consistency, which allows you to accurately time your next peek down her shirt. Oh, she'll know you're looking, but she'll wonder why she hasn't caught you at it yet.

Another good time to look is when she's preoccupied with something else (say, getting her business card out of her bag). Give an expectant look towards her hands at first, and then shift your gaze up once her attention is elsewhere. But be careful not to overindulge in the length of your look, as you're bound to get caught if you stare too long, no matter how well timed you are.

Tricks of the Trade

While you're chatting with a lovely woman, be sure to notice her other tasty traits. Many women have beautiful eyes, and looking into them can intensify a conversation. Do her eyelashes brush her cheek when she looks down? Look at her lips: Does she lick them every time right before she speaks? Can you glimpse her white teeth behind them?

If the woman is exceptionally beautiful, try to figure out what it is that makes her so lovely. Are her cheekbones classically high, her nose strikingly straight and regal? Or perhaps she has an adorable round face, with a button nose and tiny little petals for lips. How does her hair fall around her face? Is there a delicious curl behind her earlobe that you're longing to tug free? Warmer weather is a boon to the ardent girlwatcher, as less clothing means more to see. Be on the lookout for sleeveless tops, especially those with larger armholes than necessary; there are treasures to be glimpsed within. Long, straight skirts are often slit up the side or back, allowing calves and sometimes a bit of thigh to flash through. The peek-a-boo motion of this alone is enough to tease me into a frenzy.

While you're taking advantage of the heat of the sun's rays, don't forget to invest in a good pair of concealing sunglasses. Learn how to keep your head level as you follow her with your eyes alone, and you're very unlikely to get caught staring. Be sure to note nearby mirrors or reflective glass windows, allowing you to add several angles to your delicious point of view.

Body Talk

Reading her body language is an art that can be mastered only with observation, wisdom, and sometimes through a fluke innate gift. I prefer to concentrate on simply enjoying the beauty and the flow of her language, letting the meaning come when it will.

A friend put it very well in a recent note to me on this topic: "Another thing that is mesmerizing to observe is the range of movements women often unconsciously make with their legs when they are sitting down, especially when they are talking to someone they are attracted to. Some women shift their legs, in an opening and closing movement, quite dramatically if they are excited. It is fascinating, of course, because it seems like a slightly masturbatory thing to do and often one feels they are sending a signal that way. Seeing this can be quite evocative and beautiful because it leads one to think of the sensual feelings she may, quite possibly subconsciously, be getting from doing it. As a variation on this, I have also seen seated women press their hands together (as if praying, curiously enough) between their thighs and rock back and forth. Delicious."

Regardless of whether these movements come from her intense arousal or an attention deficit disorder, their meaning is negligible next to the simple beauty of observing such a dance. Watching women when they are very enthusiastic is also a treat, as the bouncing motions tend to emphasize the softness of her curves in a very feminine way.

Falling Behind

If you can, get behind her for awhile. Observing women from the rear has many benefits; the main one being that you can look at her as long as you like (until she turns around) and have only to shift your gaze from time to time to avoid being caught watching.

Long hair cascading down a supple back is enchanting, but short haircuts allow access to the neck, which causes some men I know to whimper aloud. There is something about a slender nape; if you're close enough you can see a soft down of baby hairs joining hairline with neck. If she turns her head, you can admire her profile, the line of her jaw and the crinkles of her smile.

I love noticing how the curve of her breasts flows down into the narrower valley of her waistline. A well-defined waist can emphasize the feminine fullness of her hips and buttocks, a nice place to stop and sigh before looking at her thighs through a thin skirt.

If I can, I walk behind women. Women move in so many different ways, and it thrills me to find a woman who isn't afraid to let her hips swing from side to side; this tells me that she's in a good mood, confident, and not afraid of her sexuality. That kind of confidence is arousing in people in general, but in other women, it causes me to drool.

The beauty of the "walk behind" is that you're unlikely to get caught. You can unobtrusively watch her move, delighting in every little jiggle and sway. Indeed, you can watch this way for quite some time, if you happen to be going in the same direction.

And if you're really lucky, she'll be heading off into the bright rays of the sunset.

Nearly God

Emanuel Xavier

In candlelight, I watch your Spanish eyes
staring coyly back at me
while laying naked on your bed
listening to the sounds of winds
outside South Bronx windows
shadows dancing on my olive-tanned skin
your jealous cock rises throbbing
longing to drown me
completely submerged in passion
your mother in the other room
pretending not to hear my head banging
against thin project walls
knocking knocking knocking
until our love splatters across chests and stomachs
we fall unconscious under the starry night sky
waking up the next day
to hover above you on all fours
lowering myself to the sweet intoxication of morning breath
the taste of each other lingering in our mouths
surprising your hands with black satin sheets
tying them together to return the pleasure; the pain

your mother in the other room
pretending not to hear her baby cry
ears pressed against thin project walls
St. Thérèse glistening against your Nuyorican chest
while filling in that part of you
that empty space inside
revealing love with words unspoken
with every thrust

the image of Christ pounding against the wall
crying out my name
forcing resisting muscles to open
with every groan
taking me in
completely
with all the hunger and warmth of a third world country
two bodies one
two countries united
dos almas encadenadas
prisioneros de nuestro amor
in unholy matrimony

Mad Ida Loved the Wind

Nola Summers

People still think they see Ida up on Vickery Hill whenever there's some kind of lightning storm. Think she's up there, naked to the rain and wind, arms stretched out cross-like, and long blond hair flyin'. I stopped tellin' them it weren't her. Mostly 'cause they don't listen and want to think she's there anyways. Gives 'em something to gossip about. Something to scare the kids with. I know Ida's not there 'cause I seen her walkin' outta town the other way. I never told anyone that part though. They'd just go find her, bring her back, and lock her up again. And that's not gonna help anyone, least of all Ida.

She never changed her story, not once. Loved to tell it too, just like everyone else likes to tell stories 'bout their loved ones. "Mr. Hollis, did I tell you about my special friend?"

She always started that way. Called me Mr. Hollis. My name's Hollis Green, but she called me Mr. Hollis, and talked to me just as if she was talkin' to them fancy white ladies at the country club, not some old black field worker on her daddy's farm. Sure as the sun comes up each morning, nobody ever bothered that Ida used to seek me out to talk to, 'cause they thought better me than them. Most people didn't like Ida; those country club ladies hated her.

"It was the barn door banging back and forth that woke me up, banging like it was calling my name."

She always laughed at that.

"But that's just silly isn't it. Anyway, Mr. Hollis, it was just strange. I went out to close that banging door, and that old hoot owl that lives up in the barn just stared down at me from the roof like he was expecting me. I latched it and when I was going back inside the wind just grabbed me up from behind and blew me clear out into the field."

Ida said the wind wrapped 'round her and lay her down, not lettin' her up.

"Can you imagine that? Small little gusts of wind undoing the ties of my nightgown, blowing it down and exposing my breasts to the night air. I was nearly naked, and I couldn't move. That old wind just kept me right there."

I always asked her—at about this point in her story —if surely she must have been dreaming. "Oh no, Mr. Hollis," she'd say, all offended like. Ida says she was forced over face down, her nightgown blown up and her legs lifted and spread. Now that would surely have been a sight.

"I was taken against my will. It was not my first time Mr. Hollis. I let that Lester Purdue put his thing in me a time or two, so I knew, I knew what it felt like. This was in me everywhere, filling me up and blowing across every inch of skin I have. Hot and cold, hard and soft, and sneaky, finding every avenue to get inside and fill me up. And Mr. Hollis, I have never been fuller. I never reached my peak with Lester Purdue, Lord knows Lester did, but this wind just kept blowing at me every-where and I could not help myself. I believe I saw stars before I fell back to the ground. Next thing I knew it was morning and I could hear you boys coming through the fields and I surely did not want to be found out there. As soon as I got up on my hands and knees looking for some place to hide, my Wind was back behind me, pushing in and riding me relentlessly. I simply could not move."

Ida told me her story a lot of times. Always the same, never changed a thing, and always ending it right there. "Wind's coming," she'd say, and turn with a little smile and a wink, like it was somehow our secret.

We were just headin' out early to the fields that morning, and we heard Ida before we seen her. Of course we didn't know it was her at first, but a man didn't need to have visited the whores on Canal Street to know what caused that sorta moaning. We were real surprised to find Ida over the rise; more surprised to find she was there by herself.

She was facing us on her hands and knees, nightgown twisted like a dirty rope 'round her waist. Naked but for that. Now, we were not men of the world, some had never seen a woman in the all together before, never mind a white woman, so we had a real good look see. Ida was all pale skin, pink folds, yellow hair everywhere, and near covered in mud. Her ripe little peach tits were hanging down, nipples all hard and drippin' mornin' dew. She was rockin' back and forth, eyes shut, mouth open, legs spread and shaking. There was no doubt, and not a limp dick between the four of us, that this woman was comin', and comin' hard.

It was windy in that low scoop of land. I sure didn't notice it much then, but thinking back, I recall that it was. Ida just kinda fell over then, and we stood there lookin' at her, our turn for mouths hangin' open.

We decided we'd better get her back to the big house before anyone came along and suspected somethin' else. We didn't do nothing though, didn't touch her anymore then it took to unravel that dirty nightgown, cover her up as best we could, and cart her back home. People round here thought the devil'd found Ida after that. They went from tryin' to beat it outta her to just lockin' her up. Ida got smart though. Realized if she wanted to be out runnin' round she was gonna have to keep her mouth shut and her skirts down round her knees where they belonged. Nobody'd talk to her, most would cross the street just to get away from her. Afraid the devil might find them I suppose. And I suppose that's why Ida'd come lookin' for me out in the fields. Least I'd listen to her, sometimes just so's I could get a break from workin'. But listen I did.

"You don't think I'm crazy do you Mr. Hollis?"

"No Miss Ida, I do not," I'd say. Then she'd tell me her story, just like every time before that.

"I love the Wind Mr. Hollis. And the Wind loves me."

"I know he does Miss Ida. Told me so himself just last night." That always made her smile.

Ida told me she was going to leave with the Wind one day, travel with him round the world. I didn't doubt her one bit.

I don't think her old papa ever got over the sight of his darlin' lily-white daughter being carried in the arms of four black field hands, so each night he'd lock her in this little house thing they'd built for her. She'd made so much fuss tryin' to get outta her room in the big house, wakin' everyone up all the time, that it was better for them to stick her out where they couldn't hear her.

All that kickin' and hollerin' to get out'll soon wear

down who's got to listen to it and that's how I know that's not her on Vickery Hill, 'cause I watched her walk away down that road. I let her out one night, let her out to blow around the world.

"Thank you Mr. Hollis," she said. "The Wind thanks you."

"I'm sure he does Miss Ida." I said. And off she went. Never looked back.

That was some years ago now. Long ago enough for Ida to become a bit of a story. Mad Ida they call her, say she hides up on the hill, scarin' folks every chance she gets.

Also say it ain't near as windy round here as it used to be.

Gravity

Greg Wharton

It starts with a kiss: one tender, soft kiss. We're parked out by the Henderson's old place; you know, by that house out on AA that has the billboard in the front yard, big enough for the cars traveling south on the interstate to see. ASK JESUS TO MAKE HELEN WELL. Only nobody knows who Helen is, or was.

Coal and I've just got out of work. We closed down the Dixie Queen together. It's summer: hot and boring. Just out of school, nothing going on, nothing much to look forward to but a cold beer. We drive to my house and I grab a couple six-packs of Bud from the fridge and motor down to AA where we can watch the lights of the interstate as cars drive past on their way somewhere else.

There's a bit of a breeze, and us just shooting the shit together in his beat up rusted tan Camaro. Coal and I always did get along well in school, but never talk much other than locker room lies. Then this old sappy song comes on the radio . . .

" . . . God, I miss the girl . . ."

. . . and he's babbling like a baby. Crying and saying how he doesn't understand how Deb could hurt him like she did. Deb is his girlfriend.

"Shit, Coal. I'm sorry, man. Don't cry, shit."

And I take him in my arms. It's okay; he's hurting. I take him in my arms, and squeeze. He lets me. I squeeze his strong body to mine hoping I can make him stop hurting. Before I know I'm doing it, my hands take his sweet face and pull it to mine. I kiss a tear that's slowly weeping down his cheek, then his eye. I gently run my tongue over his lips, then between to his bright white teeth, surprised at my sudden aroused state. It's like my chest is supporting a great weight, like the witches in old New England who were tortured by being laid down and having stone after stone placed on them. Only it feels good. Real good and I'm hard. I'm touching Coal and I'm hard.

He looks into my eyes. He kisses back. We kiss: one tender, soft kiss. My life is suddenly very different.

"Gravity, motherfucker! Gravity!" he yells as he bounces up from the bed on his strong legs and taps his palms on the ceiling. "Gravity."

We're so looped. A double feature at the Zucker Drive-In, two tabs of blotter acid each, and a bottle of spiced rum looped. Coal had said he wanted to fuck me in a hotel, and I'd wanted him to, so we drove to Tipp City and while he hid in the car giggling like an idiot, I got us a room.

"Come on, Vic . . . Come on! Gravity!"

I'm watching him from the other bed as he does his trampoline jumps, his fat cock bouncing up and slapping his brown tanned belly with every descent, his large heavy balls making thumping noises against his thighs. My vision is blurred; his leaps whether slowed down or speeded up I can't tell; he's just a white blur of light and motion with a hard-on.

A hard-on I want to eat. I picture it on a bed of lettuce with a slice of Wonder and a couple fluorescent pickles.

It's a week since the kiss. He had kissed me back, but then said he had to get home and drove like a bastard out of hell to get me back to my place, dropping me off and speeding away without a word about what had happened. I ran in the house, into the bathroom and jerked off, coming on the mirror above the sink in an explosion with just five quick jerks of my fist.

Nothing was said until earlier today at work when he showed me the acid and asked if I wanted to see the monster pictures at the Zucker.

"Gravity!!!" and he's suddenly flying across the room at me, knocking me off the bed with a loud thump under his full weight. His hand grips my cock through my boxers and starts pumping, keeping time with his other hand wrapped around his own.

I'm laughing, uncontrolled and hard, the effect of the drug or the rum or him. My head bends down to the plate of cock, but first I flick away the pickles. I lick the bead of come off his piss slit, then wedge the head into my mouth. Not knowing what to do with the slice of Wonder and lettuce, I fling them across the room sending trails of color with them. His cock's head seems to be larger than my mouth, but somehow I manage to make it fit.

The stinky brown shag carpet burns as we twist and bend over and around each other, but I don't care. I am too enthralled with the taste of his body, the pinpricks of sensation along my skin, his deep musky scent, like the locker room at our old school, but better. I have already come once, in his mouth. But he hasn't stopped stroking me with his lips. I have my middle finger up his ass and he is fucking hard into my throat, his knees on either side of my head, balls flapping heavily against my eyes with each thrust. His ass swallows my finger, then two. I think of my arm up inside him and then he's pulsating,

41

his cock expanding, contracting, pumping, emptying. My mind flashes greens, then blues, then bright white-silver. I think *gravity, Coal, gravity*. His fat cock finally shoots, and I know I love him. He pushes farther into me, down my throat. His come tastes like the pepperoni sausage we put on the mini-pizzas at the Queen, and I pull his thick red dick out with my hand and squeeze and it sprays my mouth and lips and tongue as I mouth *I Love You I Love You*, and his ass squeezes my fingers tight and he screams *Vic, Oh, Vic, Oh!*

For two weeks we meet every day, as best friends. As lovers. We explore each other's bodies, we talk, get high. I can't believe it, but I feel as if somebody really, finally, knows me. Nobody at work suspects the truth that two of Piqua's recently graduated have joined the ranks of the faggot brotherhood. That the king jock from Piqua High, Coal, goes down on cock: mine.

We meet before work, after work, and on nights when we close the Queen alone, we suck and fondle and paw between customers. I let him fuck me. When he shot deep inside me the first time I heard him say it. He said, "I love you, Vic." Soft and sweet as anyone could possibly say it. He didn't know it, but I cried as his cock plowed hard into my ass before exploding again within minutes of the first.

He says that he wants to go away; get out of Ohio. Maybe Chicago. That we're good together. Who cares about what people would think? He doesn't. I don't anymore.

And then it ends. No kiss. No tender soft kiss, just cold, flat words through the phone wires. He calls me on the phone and severs my life force just as if he took his favorite hunting knife and slit deep into my throat.

"Why not, man. What happened? What the fuck happened?"

"It's just over, Vic. Forget it!"

"Forget it? Coal, shit . . . I love you! I thought . . ."

"Shut up, you do not! Stop sounding like a fag, Vic! It's over!"

It's over, just like that. I pull my cock out and roughly, angrily, grind, as I think about what he said. I wrap the phone cord tightly around my balls until they look like they will burst; I start to cry. He said Deb was pregnant and wouldn't have an abortion. Somehow his dad found out and now Coal was getting married. Married! I felt like my life just ended. I want to feel his soft lips on mine again. I thought . . .

I imagine his blade forcing its way into my throat and the pain it causes. I see Deb's face smiling as he kills me, my blood flowing freely, draining.

I come all over my sneakers just as the alarm sounds, not even realizing what the alarm means. I rub the spunk from my hands on my jeans and wander out the front door staring at the sky's dark green color. My dick is hanging out and I don't care. I walk out to the cornfield in a daze.

I am peeing on the old weathered scarecrow my dad and I put up when I was nine when I first hear it. Thunder? The wind whips the stream of pee on me and I fall down yanking my jeans off, not concerned with anyone seeing just wanting to be free of them. I pull off my T-shirt and rub my hands over my chest and belly, yanking on my nipples as if I can pull them off. Nobody's around. There's never anyone around. I hate it here! I hate . . . It sounds like a train is headed right at me and a smile forms on my tear-stained face. It's a fucking tornado! Huge and black covering the entire horizon. Electricity sparkles around me and my body hair stands at attention. I watch it pick up Aunt Felice's house and devour it, then the barn across the field. I am awestruck and my cock juts out strong and stiff. Running isn't even an option. I raise my arms to the sky and think of what happened the past couple weeks with Coal. I picture his bright teeth when he smiled at me. My Coal, my love. Over. I have nothing; feel nothing. I ask Jesus to make *me* well—fuck Helen! I am lifted from the ground violently; arms spread skyward like a rocket launching, my eardrums bursting from the overwhelming roar, and I fly into my new destiny.

Gravity, motherfucker, gravity.

25 Things to Do to a Tied-Down Lover

Chris Bridges

So. You talked your lover into it, your lover talked you into it, or you both decided what the hell, and your lover is strapped down spread-eagled to the bed, helpless and waiting. *Now* what do you do? If you've fantasized about this since junior high, or if your reading habits regularly include books with titles like "Chains of Lust" or "Mistress Jones Goes to Washington," you probably have a pretty good idea where to begin and what voltage to use, but if this is your first time you might be a bit nervous. This is perfectly fine. The thing to remember is that the person you just tied down with your best scarves is now completely under your control. You decide what sensations they feel, you decide how fast or how slow to proceed, you decide when, or if, to finish. You should also decide what your ultimate goal is. Are you "just" out for the hottest sex you can whomp up, are there some domination or humiliation fantasies to consider, or are there some unresolved issues between the two of you that you're interested in addressing?

Here are some handy suggestions for what to do now that everyone's in place.

1. Kneel between your lover's legs, smiling devilishly. Make eye contact and hold it, moving your head back and forth in a hypnotic fashion. Now, quickly drop

your head to their tummy and blow loud bubbles.

2. Take the opportunity to throw out all those old clothes of his you hate.

3. Shave your lover. Make a production of it, bring out the razor and foam and hot towels and a bowl of hot water. This doesn't have to be a vital area, you could always shave his toes, or one armpit. If your lover is especially hirsute, consider shaving drawings or words into their pelt. Pubic hair, male or female, lends itself well to intriguing shapes—arrows, hearts, barcodes, palm trees, exclamation points . . .

4. Take a nap.

5. If it's torture she wants, get her strapped down good and tight and then turn on the Three Stooges Marathon. ("Commercial free, nyuk nyuk!")

6. Take the time to discuss how you really feel about your in-laws.

7. Watch a TV show and return to go down on your lover in a wildly ferocious manner during the commercials. When you hear the show starting, stop abruptly and go back to watch. See how many shows you can fit in this way.

8. Take off your own clothes, oil yourself up slowly and sensually, lay down so that you're touching your lover from shoulder to feet, then turn on the Playstation 2 and play *Medal of Honor.*

9. Light candles and let the wax drip on your lover, creating tantalizing bursts of pain-pleasure. Test it yourself beforehand to discover the optimum height to drip from without causing embarrassing emergency room visits. Experts advise using only dye-free candles; I prefer candles in loony cartoon shapes to add just a touch of levity.

10. If they're strapped down to a waterbed, bring in the garden hose, run it out the window, and start the bed

emptying. Leave.

11. Get your man erect and use his penis to catapult M&Ms into his mouth. He gets a smack on the head for every missed one.

12. Pick up the phone where your lover can hear you and call your lover's best friend to ask if they want to come over to watch videos. If you're the kind sort you can fake it and speak to the dial tone.

13. If you're not the kind sort, call your lover's parents.

14. Lay across your lover so your body covers theirs completely, and see if you can, through body undulations alone, cause them to pop a good one.

15. It is truly amazing what can be done with a water pistol full of hot water in one hand and a water pistol full of ice water in the other.

16. Pick a square inch of your lover's body and make love to it. Doesn't matter which one.

17. Invite your best friend over to help you decide what to do next. If your lover is shy, have the friend stay in the next room and call out ideas.

18. Rub a balloon across the carpet and then see if you can get every single hair on your lover's body to stand up.

19. Use your lover's body as a handy work surface. Bellies work well as mousepads (avoid the navel), firm chests make good writing surfaces, and inkpots can be balanced on the pelvic bone. Don't sneeze! Get a marker and use their body surface to make notes to yourself, to make shopping lists, to do the budget, to find the integral of $y*e^\wedge t*\arccos(xy^\wedge 2)$ with respect to x.

20. That body would also make a great serving tray. Lay out your fruits and dipping veggies, get some cold cuts and chips, and balance the dip bowl in the V of the legs. Or use it as a plate for your entrees. Eating Ramen

noodles off a collarbone is a blast. Be considerate and feed your lover occasionally, and avoid anything really uncomfortable such as prickly pears or fondue pots.

21. Kneel over their face and allow them to orally service you while you read a book. If they get too spirited (or make you lose your place) lower yourself a few inches until they calm down again.

22. Sit on the opposite side of the room and see if you can hit your lover's erect penis with a rubber band. Extra points if you get a ringer. No fair leaning forward.

23. Remember all those times you complained that he would never listen to your poetry?

24. Did you know if you place a chocolate bar on a human's chest at room temperature and they don't disturb it, it will completely melt in about an hour? Are there places on the human's body where the process might be faster? Let's find out!

25. After you're finished and your lover has been freed, lay down, spread 'em and take your turn. It's only fair.

In a Mirror, Walking Backwards

Marnie Webb

The first time I kissed a married woman was in a Taco Bell parking lot. The Taco Bell at Los Virgenes and 101, if you want to know. If you've driven past at night, up or down from Los Angeles, maybe peeling off on the twelve miles of curve that takes you from freeway to ocean, or maybe going up to Santa Barbara one Friday after work, escaping the heat of the valley during a summer weekend, then you've seen the big parking lot, dotted with artificial yellow light. We were away from the building. We'd gone through the drive-thru and were eating in the car. She had a bean burrito with cheese. I hate cheese.

In the moment before we kissed, I was talking about sailing. "I miss it," I said fumbling with my keys. "I just love being on the water so much. I can't believe I sold my catamaran." I looked up then and her face was too close to ignore. Under mine and tilted. I shouldn't have been surprised. I also shouldn't have kissed her. I know her husband. And that's just the first reason.

The moment after we kissed, I said, "You're married," which put him in the car with us. She nodded. It didn't stop us from kissing the second time.

One hand lost in her hair. With the other, I reached around her, pulled on the lever making the seat fall away and she fell back too and then was smiling up at me. "A practiced move," she said, which may have been a reason for her not to kiss me. But then I was on her side of the car, my heels bumping up against the glove box, my weight awkward and on my elbows, our legs a mixed arrangement, hers and then mine, then hers, then mine.

That kiss, the tangled-lying-back-in-the-seat kiss turned into something more. The kind of kiss women who kiss other women argue about being sex or not. I hold with a static definition: sex occurs when someone's fingers get wet. But still, talking about it, I have to acknowledge the truth. That lying down kiss was not just a kiss.

There were many things I knew that night in the Taco Bell parking lot, kissing a married woman for the first time. I knew, for example, if the Catholics were right I was writing a check for my ticket into hell. Even if only the Protestants were right I was in a lot of trouble. I knew I could never be president but that was probably true for reasons other than the kiss. I knew the best way to tell a parent that their child had a learning disability and was going to need special help. I knew the best way to get that child out of a corner of the bathroom huddled between toilet and wall because words printed on a page made no kind of sense at all. I knew intimately the way a secret could become a fearsome weight through silence and the passage of time. But I did not know the kind of secret that a married woman would become.

What else can kissing a married woman—her mouth ripe with the taste of cheap cheddar and Taco Bell fire sauce, my fingers touching her scalp, her breasts pushed against mine, my tongue tracing a figure eight on her lower lip—kissing—the passenger seat reclined in my ancient Land Cruiser, headlights from cars northbound on the 101 flashing up our bodies—what else could that be but a secret?

She said, "Are you okay with this? With this affair thing?"

"This is kissing," I said, fingers still dry, safe in my definition of sex. "This isn't an affair."

"This has been an affair for a long time," she said, palms pressing against my ribs.

And we were kissing again.

In speaking of this, I am hoping to break the spell that binds me.

Her daughter is in my class. I am an elementary school teacher, third grade. I teach volcanoes, the Chumash. I make my students do book reports. Her daughter did a shoebox diorama on Charlie and the Chocolate Factory. She'd seen the movie but not read the book. I told her mother standing in front of the school—daughter off to the side trading Pokemon cards with a friend.

She said, "Really? That doesn't sound like her. Does it sound like her to you? Are you sure?"

"I'm sure," I said. Then dropped my voice to a whisper. "I've read the book."

"I'll bet," she said and, finally, I was the one to look away.

"This has been an affair for a long time," she said, palms pressing against my ribs. I took a deep breath, expanded into her. "Miss Johnson," she said. I shifted; my elbow hit the door.

Miss Johnson is what the children in my class call me. I have twenty exactly, thanks to California laws. I buy Fiskar scissors and glue sticks. I spend lunch hour Xeroxing pages from a workbook on bears. They hug me after Spring and Winter breaks or if I've been out sick a couple of days, especially if Mr. Tibbor is their substitute. All the kids hate Mr. Tibbor. I don't blame them.

They run up to me, the children in my class, and say, "Where have you been Miss Johnson?" And then they hug me. Not just the smart girls who read well and do their homework neatly and, I'm fairly sure, with their parents' help. But Sean, too. The boy who cannot read and I'm trying to get him into some kind of program, convincing his parents to get him into something where he can get more time than I have in a classroom of twenty kids all reading poems about bears. We call February *Febu-bear-y* in my class. They are young enough that even the boys think this is cute. The parents think I am clever. I do not tell them I stole the idea from a third grade teacher I worked with at my last school. March is just March in my class. We only get cute with *Febu-bear-y*.

I've had parent-teacher conferences. Both she and her husband crouched into child chairs. He is tall and had to turn sideways, knees unable to fit under the desk. I told them their daughter was doing well which was true. I had no reason to lie. She and I weren't kissing at that point.

Do not think I'm going to tell you any names. Sure, Mr. Tibbor, who deserves what he gets after he told Sean to shut up. In those words, something a teacher should never do. And the only noise Sean makes in class is when he cries. That's one of the things that worries me about him. And Sean, I'll give you him, and maybe even the old third grade teacher from whom I stole *Febu-bear-y*. Mrs. Addy. How's that? She probably had to be a third grade teacher. That's probably the deal that went with the name. But the daughter, the husband, and the woman I kissed. Those names I keep to myself. You might know her. Infidelity is a deal breaker. I don't want to hurt her life.

We did more than kiss. It became sex by anybody's

definition. Not that night in that parking lot. Later. After we'd made the decision to see each other again. Premeditated. That makes it worse, right? The point at which we began planning.

Do not think this is all of my life. Teaching eight-year-olds cursive and giving spelling tests. Having sex with the married mother of one of my students. There are other parts which are separate.

Separate does not mean better. It means there are lines in my life which are crossed by no one but me.

That is the most frightening thing about the married woman I kissed in the Taco Bell parking lot. She exists in more than one segment of my life. I see her not just when I am lover, but when I am teacher as well. This collision of selves makes me dizzy.

My family is another part of my life. There are no lines I allow them to cross. They see me only in corners of rooms, wine glass raised, wishing someone a happy birthday, anniversary, pulling out a funny story—the one again about the plum jam that exploded in hot splashes of purple on my grandmother's stove leaving such a mess she had to mop the ceiling, wash all the curtains— laughing with a cousin I see once a decade. My family thinks I am funny. They cannot see me running a class-room. They do not see in me the gentle head down, my hand on Sean's shoulder trying through touch to transfer the ability to read. I let him struggle with a word until it hurts me too and then I sound it out slowly, my finger on the page. I can feel the heat from his face on the inside of my arm. I stoop to be close to him. I say, "You're better at math than anyone I know." This is true. It is also true that no one in my class of third graders cares about math. Maybe I'll make a math project. Maybe I'll give them a forest of bears and trees and food and then word problems. If there is one bear in each tree and there are fourteen bears and five empty trees, how many trees are there in the forest? It's April but I'll give it to them anyway. I'll ask them the question aloud. Sean will raise his hand. The daughter will, too, but to ask what kind of trees they are.

My family does not see in me that I can care so much about someone. As much as I care about Sean. As much as I care about the married woman I kissed.

I try to keep it from being so wrong. I call her the woman I kissed.

We went out again. Made plans standing on the grass in front of the school, a slow line of Suburbans and Volvos, mini-vans, her daughter holding her hand. We made plans to see a movie.

I had seen it before and bought popcorn and coke, only one of each so we had to share. She was inside getting seats.

Through the movie I thought only of the touch of our shoulders, of the coke she kept on the far side so that I had to reach across her body to get it. Casual, constant contact.

At dinner, we both ate French dips and this is something I like about her. I said, "I'm so glad you're not a salad eater."

"I am," she said and poured the Italian dressing onto the side of salad on my plate.

"This is kid salad," I said pushing the iceberg around, chunk of tomato, pile of grated carrot. "We have this in the cafeteria."

In a curved booth, one bench fitted around three sides of a table, we sat at the base of the U. My legs stretched in front of her. Her feet on the seat, the top of one bare foot pressing into my thigh. My voice would fall and she would lean into me, her shoulder between my breasts, hair thick against my mouth and nose. "What," she would say.

I have said I know the cost of secrets.

Here is one I have kept: I am a lesbian. I have kept it from my family. I have kept it from colleagues. I have kept it from the parents of my students. Until this woman, I have kept it from the parents of my students. I am a lesbian dancing in bars. Turning on the floor. I sing the words to a Madonna song. I sing, "I feel like a disco ball." The song is out for months before I know the words are really "I feel like I've just come home." I have only felt the disco ball way. Shattered and spinning. Light bouncing off my body in a dappled mix of colors. A whiskey tonic on the ledge by the mirror as I spin and spin. Later, in a car, my hands running up the sides of some woman, looking into her face, trying to identify the second of desire. Holding myself back to see her as she forgets herself. Forgets that I am watching. It does not happen every time that these anonymous women forget themselves in pleasure. It almost never happens that I do.

And when I leave them, driving home, tired, the muscles in my forearms trembling and sore, going down the coast road into my own home town, a private distance from the places where I dance, I slide back into the person that the geography of teacher demands.

My mother says, "Why aren't you married?" She points to my younger cousin, a zoologist with the San Diego Zoo, holding her husband's hand, a tall beefy man who works in construction. "Gracie's seven years younger than you are."

This happens every time I am with them.

"I like my space."

My mother has never been in my home. Neither has my brother.

"I do not like children," I tell my family. They believe me. I do not touch my cousin's child. I stand

55

in the corner, wine glass in hand. I prefer Merlot. Pinot Grigio during the summer. It is a joke, with my family, that I am an elementary school teacher.

"What kind of career choice," my brother always says.

"I thought about being a pediatrician," I always answer.

"The only thing worse," my brother says.

It is not hard for me to stay silent about the married woman I am kissing. I am practiced. It is the kind of secret I am used to keeping. I know its cost. The hesitations before the hugs from my family. The serious conversations that stop as I enter the room.

I cannot speak of the married woman directly. She is so hidden, nestled inside me. I worry standing outside the school with her that it will show when I look at her. Lost and forgetting what I am supposed to say next. I must always distort. Looking at her out of the corner of my eyes, at the ground first, flexing my fingers and looking at the grass through the space between them. And smile and when I look up at her I am caught in a delicious moment which contains all of my possible selves and none of them. Caught as teacher and lover at once. I am afraid.

After the French dips and my cafeteria salad, we drove in lazy, city-wide circles. One looping freeway into another. I kept both hands on the steering wheel. I was afraid of what would happen in a parked car.

"A hotel," she said. "We're both adults. We have credit cards."

I pulled into a Ramada Inn. Her hand on my thigh. The heat of her palm through my jeans. I could not remember the last time I had been in a bed with someone, having sex somewhere other than my car.

Inside the room, we stood, nervous space between us. She touched my face. "Does this mean you'll pass my kid?"

"She's already passing," I said and then realized it was a joke.

Her hand on my face, palm light against my chin, fingers playing at my hairline, against my ear. Her thumb at the corner of my mouth.

I will not tell you what she looked like. That would give her away as surely as her name. But even alone I had to close my eyes against the desire I had for her, against the heat rising through my body. Maybe when I say that you get some idea.

The distance between us, her arm's length. I could not move toward her. There would be no stopping me, I thought, after the first step. After the first touch, alone in a motel room. We could hear the shushurah of cars speeding past. Heavy curtain pulled, we stood in a shadowed darkness. The picture over the bed, I was sure, was bolted to the wall. The red numbers of a digital clock, and, though I tried to mark the passage of time, I never saw the numbers change. Behind me, I didn't need to turn, would be a dresser, wide and low, with TV and mirror.

If I stepped toward her, pulled her against me, breasts, ribs, knobs of her spine against my arms, hair in my mouth, breathing in a want of her, I would have no resources with which to stop myself. No resources to draw upon standing on the grass waiting with my children for their parents to come, their nannies, their older brothers. I would not be able to speak to Sean's mother, to say again, "I have too many students. That's the only thing. He needs more attention." And I'd see in her face, again, that to put her son in a special program would be a failure. "If he gets it now," I'd say. "You have no idea how smart that boy is. I have no idea how smart that boy is."

She would be standing on the grass next to me, my married woman, Sean holding my hand and laughing at some joke I pulled out of the air for him. A whispered comment. Teachers always have favorites. My married woman next to me. Sean still laughing; his mother looking at me as if I am an insult. My married woman next to me would overwhelm all other possibilities. My desire for her would be as great there as in the hotel room, alone, where there was no need for secrets.

The bed wide behind her, my eyes adjusted to the dark. The picture was a seascape. "A nursing home picture," I said.

She stepped into me, turned, shoulder between my breasts, ear at my mouth. My own hot breath reflected back at me. "What?" she said. She turned her mouth to my throat.

"Over the bed," I said but still low. Her lips harder against me. I felt the echoing buzz of my voice. My hands traveling her. Up her stomach, cupping her breasts. "The kind of picture they have in nursing homes," I said.

"I want you." A directness I could not answer.

She moved away from me and to the bed. Peaked and stormy ocean wave above her. Oil so thick it was raised from the canvas. Clock at her shoulder. The numbers changed, but I had lost their relationship with time.

She closed her eyes.

I cannot do this, I thought, and turned away. In the mirror, in the dark bubble of TV screen, I saw her reflected.

Picture, clock, bed.

I thought, I can move toward her looking in a mirror, walking backwards.

She opened her eyes and I turned, crossing the room, three easy steps, and fell in with her. All parts of me moving at once. She laughed, head back. Lost with her.

Selves converged.

The secret Sean's mother tries vainly to keep is that her son, already eight, cannot read. I know the cost of this secret but it is Sean who suffers the price. In the hotel room, I lost myself. Lines have been crossed and there is no going back. My married woman is too bound up in me now. Concealing her, I conceal myself as well.

This is the kind of secret the married woman has become: the kind of secret I cannot keep.

I do not know how I will stand in the corner—winter Merlot, summer Pinot Grigio—repeating the same stories to my cousins, ten years older. Trading the same comments, as if they were new, with my brother. And when my mother asks why I am not married, I do not know how I will avoid the truth.

And on the lawn, Sean in hand, waving as children open the back doors of cars that seat more people than my dining room table, their backpacks slung over one shoulder, ready for music lessons, swimming lessons, soccer and tutors that round out every scheduled second of their day, I do not know how I will keep from hugging Sean against me, saying *You are the smartest person I know* and telling his mother she is the stupidest.

My married woman, tapping an impatient foot for her daughter, fully in my sight.

I Didn't Want

Jim Tolan

I didn't want
to fuck you in the burned-out building
last night because, in your long purple dress, new
European shoes, and nothing else to complicate
the finery of your heroic flesh, I wanted you
moonlit on a featherbed with oils and no rush,
wanted my tongue to move over you till dawn
and not splash your thighs before the sun
called us out of doors. I didn't want to fuck you
in a burned-out building because I wasn't ready
to share you with the sky, the curious eyes
of the moon and stars. I didn't want to fuck you
in the burned-out building because I was not
man enough to come out loud with pants
around my ankles, my hands cradling
your firm ass in the empty window sill,
because I was scared to want you riding me
beside roach shit and the malt liquor stench,
scared to want my tongue between your legs
as you leaned against a smoke-stained wall.
I didn't want you in the burned-out building
because there was nothing I wanted more,
because I wasn't ready to give up your scent
to the wind, because my cock would have been

so hard our screams would have brought the cops,
because our juices would have drowned your fine
new shoes, because we would have burst into rain
and you are too hard to find beneath the earth,
because we've waited long enough to find each other
solid and almost whole. I didn't want to fuck you
that lost and randy night awhirl with possibilities
because I am an idiot of lyric proportions.

All I Want is Everything

Jane Duvall

I. On the Twenty-Fourth Floor

I don't remember opening the door, walking in, how I ended up on the bed. Did he shove me down? Had I laid down? Do the details matter, when what does matter is that somehow he was undressed, over me, intense, wanting to hurt me? I was fighting back, though not entirely in earnest. Just that touch of fear when I know it will be too much, too hard to take. He got up, got the rope, and tied my legs, the muscles in his forearms flexing with the effort it took to subdue me all the way. Once the choice was gone, I fell into it as I always do, no longer afraid, no longer caring about pain, reveling in the beauty that this chemistry between us created. And later, on top for once —which I usually hate—not noticing the effort, not caring if my legs were tired, just moving with abandon. Being the cause of too much sensation is usually a hard state for me to reach, but I loved fucking him, arching back to feel him as deeply as I possibly could.

Later, I fell into a nap the second he untied me, waking only to the sounds of him showering. He was going to snap a few photos of me outside the room, so I got up while he was gone to take my own shower and get ready for the photos—ostensibly the purpose of our little jaunt together.

I thought I was good and rested by then, but it was amazing how quickly I dropped the second the rope touched my skin. Laying on the chaise lounge, being picked up and carried across the room, then back again. I became the most patient model in the world, even though I was spent from our earlier interlude, and before I knew it I was once again entwined in hemp.

We were in bed that night by eleven p.m., and I was asleep first, unable to keep my eyes open as soon as my head hit the pillow. There was nothing sweeter than going to sleep with his hand gently stroking my hair as he watched television next to me.

In the morning it was serious photo time. Photos taken in front of the windows, twenty-four floors up. My very real fear of heights kicked in, and once I was tied there I had to focus just to get through it. Breathe in, breathe out . . . think of anything but looking down.

This sparked his sadism. I'd thought we were through with anything right by the windows once my legs were untied, until he pulled me by the hair over to the windows, pushing me toward the glass, arms still firmly bound behind my back. I panicked, screamed, and was genuinely terrified, until he let me fall to the floor at his feet. Then I was crying, my face pressed against his legs as he stood above me.

It wasn't the kind of play that does anything for me in a sexual sense. But it was cathartic to cry, and I like it when that happens. I love knowing that he's turned on by the sight of my tearstained face. I suppose it's a different kind of submission to be okay with him tormenting me that way. He wanted to, so he did. That's enough for me, just that he wanted to. In his own way, his brand of D/s is far deeper than things I've done before. It's not flowery, it's not ritualized, but he points out to me all the time that in the big ways I have let myself become his. He points out that he can do things to me just because he feels like it, no negotiation.

Before we knew it, it was noon and we were hungry. We walked out into a very windy day, windy enough that it felt like Chicago instead of Seattle. My hair was whipping around, getting tied in knots. I was so depleted from the morning shoot that I had about two brain cells left and couldn't hold a thought. Thankfully he took care of everything, finding us a cab, finding us a diner, getting calories into my system—eggs benedict, my favorite.

I packed my things while he was out taking more cityscape photos, then collapsed on the chaise for a tiny nap. I woke up to the sight of him taking my picture from the entry of the hallway. The camera so rarely leaves his hands. Twenty-four hours after I picked him up, I was dropping him back off, with just a hint of sadness that this weekend was already over.

II. Master Bath

When he said he wanted to do bathtub pictures, I was okay with it, since I love my clawfoot tub. He was in there, checking out the lighting, while I looked for something to wear—not that rope isn't a fine outfit in and of itself. But I came across some little white lace panties, and I knew he'd love the contrast with the black patent knee-high lace-up boots I was wearing.

I walked into the bathroom to ask what he thought, and his appreciative gaze made me realize I'd guessed right. The shoots I liked best were the ones where he was distracted enough by his own arousal that a definite pause would have to happen.

It started innocently enough, although I felt a little silly sitting on the edge of my bathtub in the boots. But knowing he liked the shots he was getting was really all that mattered. By the sink, putting on lipstick in the mirror . . . but then I started to balk when he wanted photos sitting on the toilet. Yet I went with his instructions with as little sulking as I could manage.

We must have shot a hundred photos before he decided he was ready to do rope. I was longing for it by then, because I so love the feel of hemp on my skin, and the feel of his hands on me as he ties. I looked down and saw his strong forearms and hands on my breasts, and threw my head back, gasping when he decided to grab a nipple and squeeze. Yes, I was definitely ready for his rope and whatever he decided would follow. The intensity of our relationship seemed to grow every time I saw him, and I was falling right into his energy, without even a tiny bit of wanting to hold back.

Rope wound around my torso and my breasts, and then he was tying knots that would lie right against my clit. He pulled it up roughly between my legs, tying it awfully snug. Within five minutes of the rope coming out, there I was, already lost. When I could manage to look up, it was with lust and yearning. I relished the intensity of his gaze, loving it more when I noticed that he was a bit lustful too.

Then he lifted me into the bathtub. I knew what he wanted, it was all about the cold hard surface of the cast iron tub. I knew it would start to hurt in no time at all, lying there tied like that. And that he'd wait and watch, and that he'd be hoping to bring me to tears. I felt my body sink into it, hurting. I could picture a bruise forming under the surface of my skin, on the shoulder that was bearing so much of my weight. But I knew this type of torture, I knew that if I tried to adjust the position I'd only hurt more. It was a waiting game. I'd look up, see those intent, dark eyes on me, and hold his gaze, letting him see my pain. I liked to suffer for him, for the knowledge that it was turning him on.

He wasn't shooting photos then, he was waiting patiently—and enjoying his own arousal, his hand going to his erection. I wanted him so badly, but I was bound, waiting, helpless, and there was nothing to be done but watch.

I was almost to tears by the time he came to lift me out, and as he grabbed hold of the ropes and lifted me into the air, there was a burst of pain, all centered on the crotchrope which had gotten so tight that I was sure my entire vulva was one big bruise. I lay there on the floor at his feet, gasping, trying to catch my breath from that unexpected pain. He let me recover a bit, then pulled me up to my knees. Quickly, he wound rope around my eyes and face. Then his voice again, that I've been trained so well to respond to, said—*Open*. My mouth opened, needing him—I didn't know at the time that the camera was still out, until I saw the images later.

He was more controlling when it came to oral than anyone I'd ever been with before. And I enjoyed it more with him than I ever had with anyone else. Before it was always a thing just done to please my partner. I was never into it totally, but whether it was intentional on his part or not, I felt like I was slowly morphing into a total oral service slut. Was it calculated? Is that what he wanted of me? I didn't mind, although I wanted other things too— like the sting of his whip, the feel of his cock deep inside me . . . everything. I always end up wanting everything.

Soon enough, the camera was forgotten. It was an odd thing to be photographing our own personal sex life, and I liked when I could draw him in deep enough that he just couldn't take another photo until his lust had been sated. And it was.

In the last photos in the shoot I look so very forlorn there on the bathroom floor. Wanting his hands on me, wishing for more play instead of more photos. Soon the rope was coming off (I always hate that time, I'm never ready for it to come off), and he was putting me into bed, holding me close. I was still a wreck, though, and I wanted him to fuck me so badly. I didn't want him to put me on a plane bound for Chicago in that state. I knew I'd just die of longing while I was gone if he did.

He took pity on me, pushed me back, tied ankles to thighs and fucked me with a dildo from the bedside drawer. Hard, so hard—no time to catch my breath. I guess I'd asked for it—begged for it, really. The hardest part was him making me use it to fuck myself while he watched. I'd never been able to masturbate in front of a partner before. But he was coercive, hurting my nipples enough every time I stopped so that I'd continue, tentatively, until I finally begged for him to let me be done.

I still wanted *him,* not that silicone substitute, but that weekend ended in wanting and knowing I'd have to wait. I will see him again soon—will he be merciful then? I so hope that he doesn't just tease me and send me home. I don't think I can bear it again.

Drums

Jeff Beresford-Howe

"Come hear Uncle John's band
By the riverside
Got some things to talk about
Here beside the rising tide"

Wandering back from a long, dissonant, confused jam to tight, three-part harmony. Unity and strength, and especially redemption after a long, hard journey. The voices still, then silence, but for just one beat. The drummers begin the tribal stomp, the planet drum. First one then the other take up the ritual as the other members of the band leave the stage. You feel my hand on the small of your back guiding you to a position in front of me. You face away from me and toward the stage, your back against my chest, your long hair falling over my shoulders. My hands caress your rolling, sexy hips, hips that move the way only a woman who knows sex can make them move. My touch is light because I don't want you to stop.

One of my hands slides up your back and lifts your hair, exposing the back of your neck, and I begin to nibble and gently bite you there. I hear you sigh, and I press my mouth harder against you. Your ass is brushing against my jeans now, and you can feel me harden against you. It just makes you dance harder. You love feeling me get hard.

I take your wrists in my hands and lift your arms up over your head, behind you and behind my neck. You grind harder against my cock, approving of your new position, but you don't moan until a moment later, when I tell you to clasp your hands behind my neck. Your hands come together and you're now stretched out against my body. I can touch you anywhere. As the two drummers play, I play you, touching, stroking, petting, pinching under your loose dress. My hands find your nipples and stroke them until they're hard against my palm. I start pinching, playing your nipples like drums, small hard drums that need a firm stroke. You're breathing hard now, trying not to draw attention to yourself but lost in my arms, lost to the music, lost against my body.

As you grind against me, you feel one of my hands move down across your belly, between your legs. You're soaking wet. My hand moves along the length of your pussy, sliding easily, stroking you, but always stopping short of where you want me to touch you. You grind harder, hoping your ass will entice my cock to take care of you, but I whisper, "No, just hold on to me," and you do.

I resume stroking you, always just missing where you want me to be, and you're aching for me now, aching to be touched. The crowd suddenly starts to get intensely loud as one of the drummers holds a huge baton out toward the audience. The audience knows he's asking for their assent to pound the huge drum suspended behind him, and 15,000 people start yelling it all at once. The crowd's screams get louder, my hand works faster and faster, and suddenly time slows down . . .

everything is happening at once, too fast to name or under-
stand . . .

you realize that my hand is on your clit . . . when did that
happen?

you see the baton approach the gong . . .

you feel my cock against your ass . . .

you feel your nipples so hard against your dress . . .

you feel my mouth against your neck . . .

you feel yourself stretched and open to me . . .

you see the edge of the stick baton strike the gong . . .

you come

lost lost lost little girl

the gong seems to ripple . . .

the sound ripples out over the audience, you can see the
wave . . .

your orgasm ripples through your body . . .

your legs get weak, but I'm holding you up, rocking you
gently

You see the stage and the drummers are gone and the rest
of the band is playing a sweet space elegy, hot and loose and
everywhere at once, and you float with it, float with me. With
your dream, your drummer, your lover for life.

Big

Rachel Kramer Bussel

It's simple—big girls and guys make me weak in the knees. They make me swoon, because I know they'll be there to catch me. They make me want to lay down for them, strip, seduce, submit, proffer myself to them. And I do, again and again and again.

I'm 5'2" and curvy, but there's no exact weight or height you need to be in order to pass my "big" test. It's more a matter of knowing it when I see it. The fact is, most people are bigger than me in some way. But I want more than that; I want substance and confidence, someone who is a natural leader to guide my submissive erotic soul. Sometimes I go for curvy, feminine dominant women, who can get me into that cowering, submissive space in seconds. Other times big burly guys, who to me are like tough teddy bears, do it for me. When I curl up against a big guy, I instantly feel calm, safe, warm. I know that he will make me feel protected and special. With a big guy, I can bury my head in his neck or arm or chest—any part of him really—and feel protected. Sometimes big guys worry that they will hurt me if we have sex in positions where they're on top, but as long as I have breathing room, I relish the feeling of being immobilized during sex.

Big girls do that for me too, full of warmth and softness and curves. And if they're also a little mean, I get the best of both worlds. I like dominant women, especially the way they wield their power with a seductive smile that turns into a snarl, the way they look so good holding an implement of torture. I like the way they can summon up all the bad girls and she-devils of history with one commanding word. I like the play of opposites, my smaller submissive self to their larger dominant self; it's like finding my other half. I also learn from my larger female lovers about loving and being proud of my own body. I met a tough, bold, funny, adorable femme at a sex party; she was wearing a black bra and panty set featuring flames, along with shoes to match. She was happy to be decked out in an outfit that had required a lot of care to acquire (the shoes were purchased on Ebay), and stood so boldly and confidently I was instantly drawn to her. She wore her size with such ease, grace and toughness, and flirted with me so shamelessly, that I was not only attracted to her, but also awed by her. Many other larger women I've slept with have had a confidence that I think is tied to their size, and that makes them seem even stronger and more powerful. I get the sense that they won't put up with any bullshit, from me or anyone else, that they'll protect me and also take me to my erotic edge, and be there to catch me if I fall.

To me, a rounded belly has the kind of sexual symbolism that large breasts have for some people; I love to rub my hands up and down a large belly. Sometimes this garners me strange looks, even from the large person themselves; they don't always understand why I want to stand in front of them and rub their naked belly, probably because that rarely happens to them. But for me, bellies are extremely erotic, and it's not the same if they're too flat. I like to rub my cheek against the curve of a swelling stomach, breathing hotly onto it before I move up or down.

I also think that, contrary to myth, erotic allure springs from charm and confidence, not from possessing the body type of the moment. I had a good friend, D., who was very fat and didn't seem to be too bothered by it. He worked behind the counter of a record store and had vast knowledge about all sorts of music. When he talked about music, he came alive, and I'd pass by his store on my way home from grad school and talk to him almost every day. He'd play me his favorite records and regale me with musical trivia and make plans to go see local bands. I wasn't head over heels for him the first time I met him, but as I got to know him, he became more and more attractive, and the truth is, he got lots of girls because he was just so exciting and interesting. That's not to say he was attractive despite his body, but I think his size and general indifference to his appearance made him blend in, so the attraction could sneak up on you. All of a sudden, I'd realize that after my daily talk with him I was turned on. While we were never lovers, I could easily see myself being intimate with him.

The "big" dynamic is also a very important part of my BDSM play. In order to bottom to someone, or even have good vanilla sex with them, I like to feel just a little vulnerable. I want to feel like I might be getting myself into something a little frightening, a little dangerous.

And especially if I'm bottoming to someone, I need to believe that whatever scary plans they've cooked up or verbalized could really happen. I need to know that if they really wanted to, they could hurt me, just by their sheer physical strength. And largeness is actually a double-edged pleasure, because while it gets me wet to be on that edge of fear, a big gal or guy is there to comfort me when I need it.

There's nothing like folding myself into a ball after having gone through a vulnerable or nerve-wracking scene and having someone wrap their arms around me and engulf me. I love burrowing into a warm neck or shoulder or stomach, getting lost in the other person's skin and smell.

One former lover, A., is an incredibly voluptuous woman who wears her body so well she would look odd at any other size. She's not fat by any means but she's definitely well rounded, at least to my mind, and yet I wouldn't describe her as soft. On some women, being large and curvy makes them seem maternal, soft, delicate. She looked tough and dangerous, and combined with her no-nonsense talking and fondness for spanking, she was gorgeous and enticing. But I also found that even though she didn't look soft on the outside, in bed with her I did find warmth, comfort and sweetness. One morning while I was visiting her, after we'd both been up very late, we spent the morning tucked into bed under her covers, talking and sleeping curled up together, all arms and legs and lingerie entwined atop her bed high off the ground. That morning was so special to me, because I got to see another side of her, different than the tough girl who walks down the street like she owns it, different than the girl who stands guard and can get a decidedly evil look on her face. This was the side of her that goes along with her very sweet, high voice, her girlish laugh, and the grin that can light up not just her face but her entire body.

In my sexuality, I look for ways to lessen the control I like to have in my daily life. Daily, I spend too much time worrying, fretting, thinking, going over my to-do lists. With sex, I don't want to have to do that. It's not that I don't want to have to think or plan or be alert, but I don't want to be in charge. I definitely want to be an active participant, even when I'm bottoming, but I want to know that my partner is ultimately the one leading the way.

I went to a class recently by Fetish Diva Midori, and she asked us what the two things we absolutely need out of a scene are. This way, you can identify whether you and another potential player will possibly click, or whether you have no hopes for having a mutually satisfying scene.

This was an idea I hadn't considered before, usually taking my play on an individual case by case basis, but it proved interesting to ponder. While many of my needs are variable and depend on the person and situation, one of mine would definitely have to be this physical factor. Playing with a larger partner sets me at ease and makes me feel more comfortable with my body and with theirs. I know that they are physically strong enough to truly intimidate me, and I hope that they have learned how to harness and truly know their own strength and power as a Top.

Another thing I need is to really trust a person to play with them, and preferably have played with them privately before playing publicly. Though that might seem like a given, for me that trust usually takes time, which is why you'll rarely find me hooking up or playing at a party with someone I've just met. Flirting yes, but playing has to wait. It's not always easy for me to know how far I'll want to go or how much I can trust someone, so I often have to play things by ear, but I can only do that when I feel that the person I'm playing with is 100% trustworthy, and then I can relax and let my desires lead me.

While having a partner larger than I am definitely helps get me in the mood, I don't look around a room and try to find the biggest person there; it's usually not until I'm flirting with someone that it hits me that their big body is part of their appeal. Again and again, seemingly by accident, I'm drawn to people who are bigger than me in some way.

Even if they don't tower over me, they may be physically stronger or weigh more than me. I don't want to be able to arm wrestle or beat them up; they should win those contests. I want to be at their mercy, and I want us both to know it. When I'm not, usually with women, it's not that I don't enjoy it, but I find myself in another role than the one I'm used to. I'm more likely to take charge, to initiate sexual activity, to be more top than bottom, if I'm larger than the other person. I can't say I haven't enjoyed those times, but it's definitely not the same, and I find myself missing having a larger partner.

It feels a bit odd to state that so boldly, because it's not every big person that I'm attracted to, but most people I seriously lust after are pretty amply sized. I know that I can let go with them, that they will take care of me on some basic, elemental level that I need to feel at ease. I don't have to be the one worrying about whether they had a good time during sex, because I trust them to do what they need to do to make that happen. I can let the "worry" part of my mind go during sex and just be free to enjoy it, which in turn makes it better for both of us because I can get more into pleasing them. Making a big lover come is such a thrill because it's like having won a prize or caught an elusive prey; just by my sexual magic I can get this big, beautiful person to stop what they're doing and enjoy my ministrations.

I don't want to feel completely weak and helpless, but I want my feelings of weakness and helplessness to be enhanced and dramatized. Even if it's all in my head and never told to my lover, I like knowing that they are bigger and stronger. I want to feel vulnerable, I want my partner to make me a little on edge, I want to be caught unaware. I want there to be times when I don't know exactly what they're capable of.

And I want to revel in that uncertainty, to know that if they wanted to hurt me, they could. I don't just want that, I need that, otherwise BDSM play is all too unreal to me. When I know that they can physically overpower me, that if they wanted to hold me down, they could by their sheer strength, I get wet. And afterwards, being with someone bigger makes the entire experience better. Cuddling against them, the way their arms wrap around me calms me down and makes me feel safe, protected and beautiful.

So what could I put in my potential personal ad, the one that always lays half-written in my head? That's not easy, because I'm not looking for a standard "type," not blondes or redheads or leather daddies or software engineers. Maybe it comes down to this: I want someone big enough to give me what I need, and then some.

After Bill

Dorothy Bates

On the job at Independence Movers,
you were the strongest of all the guys.
I've seen you climb six flights of stairs
with a refrigerator strapped to your back.

I never told those guys that after work
you wore my high-heeled pumps
and stretched them into ruins.
I never told them that you set free your
ponytailed hair, snapped tiny metal clamps
on your nipples, wore black lace panties
with the back cut out and tied back
your sex with a leather thong.
I never told them that your secret name
for yourself was *Sweet Billy Buns*.

You were the Fourth of July in bed, honey.
I told them that.

Tennis Turn-Ons

Naomi Darvell

All summer long I obsess about tennis. I play every chance I get; even more fanatically, I watch. During Grand Slam tournaments, I've been known to stay by the TV all day just to see the live matches stroke for stroke.

While I enjoy all tennis action, what really rocks my world is women's tennis. Those gorgeous women hitting, jumping, spinning, grunting, and yelling with effort and emotion. That moment before the serve, when the player receiving leans over and shifts her weight from one foot to the other, looking ready to take off. It's exhilarating to watch, and more: It turns me on.

Tennis has always had erotic potential. A friend of mine explains what he likes about the sport:

"Those short skirts with tennis panties underneath. I remember a woman pro caused a scandal years ago by wearing frilly panties under her skirt. And then there is the fact that tennis players have killer legs and round bottoms."

Girly-girly tennis outfits aren't in style now; if anything, the players look sexier to me in sleeker costumes. I confess I love the big powerful women: Jennifer, Lindsay, Amélie, Serena, and especially the aptly-named Venus. Venus is slimmer, a little more reserved than her sister. Serena blows away her competition with sheer intensity; Venus has a more quiet, calculating kind of power. Whether she's winning or losing, she smiles like she has a secret. No matter who else is on the court, I can't take my eyes off her.

My sexual attraction to tennis used to embarrass me some. This year, I realized how many people feel the same. The French Open finals, on U.S. TV, came along with a montage of the Williams sisters playing to the tune of "Voulez-vous Coucher Avec Moi?" from the Moulin Rouge sound track. Kind of a weird choice, but it seemed like a big nod to the erotic element of the game.

Then, during Wimbledon, everyone got hot and bothered over a wire photo of Anna Kournikova kissing Tatiana Panova, who'd beaten her in the first round. It was an amazing picture. Kournikova was probably going for Panova's cheek, but an accident of the camera angle made it look like the beginning of a real open-mouthed smooch. Kournikova was smiling; Panova's face was in shadow. You could see the sweat on both women's skin. A flukey shot, and sort of a male "lesbian" fantasy, but I liked it anyway. It brought out, for me, what an intimate game tennis is. It's a physical and mental duel; you're deeply engaged with your opponent.

The cerebral quality of tennis—the strategy, the psyching, the close engagement—adds an edge to the sexiness. It's combative, unpredictable. In John Updike's novel *Couples*, a character muses about tennis: "A fluid treacherous game. Advantages so swiftly shifted. Love became hate." Watching a good tennis match can be like watching a madly passionate affair in two or three sets.

Wimbledon is my favorite Slam. It's smack in the middle of summer. The players wear all white, which has a retro appeal. (The purity of white really added to the buzz of the famous Panova-Kournikova picture.) Most of all, Wimbledon means . . . Martina!

Navratilova is a fantastic commentator. She gets right inside the players' heads, and she feels what's going on in their bodies. Of one player, who doesn't seem quite "on," she says, "Her body hasn't flown yet. She needs to run to be happy." You can tell she's speaking from her own experience. She also makes her frank appreciation of the players clear, praising a contestant who stands "tall, strong, and confident." She's never suggestive; she just conveys sensuous love of the sport.

Martina's commentary doesn't gloss over a certain brutality in tennis today. "She broke her," she'll say tersely when one player has broken another's serve. And she remarks ruthlessly: "Small doesn't cut it. Everyone who's winning is big." (That is sad. Personally I wish there were more room for lightness and finesse as well as Amazonian power at the very top, but that doesn't mean I can't adore the Amazons.) When she speaks of a player doing well, she says, "She's dominating."

"Dominating" is a good word. For a kinky type like me, tennis pushes a lot of buttons. It's not just the intense, sweaty struggle. There's something particular about the skills and energy involved. A fellow BDSMer (male variety) told me:

"I know that women's tennis has always resonated for me . . . my father briefly tried to teach me tennis and he used to describe the forehand stroke as paddling someone's bottom, since you are supposed to use the kind of flat arc on the forehand swing that you would to paddle someone bent over a desk."

Whew! That image crosses my mind a lot, when I'm watching one of my favorite players whack a ball.

By now it's obvious that I revel in the erotic displays of center court. But it has to be admitted, there has been a backlash against the sexualization of women's tennis. This summer, Jeanette Winterson wrote in the *Guard-*

ian:

"Men are allowed to be sex symbols and serious tennis players. Women have to make a choice. Anna Kournikova is nothing like as good at the game as the Williams sisters, but until recently she could play tennis. Now all she can do is get knocked out of Wimbledon and read the papers about her lost career."

She goes on to say that messages about Kournikova's sex appeal have undermined her game. "Concentrating on her body is a way of keeping her in her place."

In my opinion, Winterson is dead wrong. One thing that makes tennis so sizzling, for me, is that unlike stereotypically sexy sports like figure skating and gymnastics, it doesn't give any points for appearance. Yes, tennis rewards size these days, which could be a problem for the game. But for women's images, how refreshing is it that a lot of the stars are big and far from wasp-waisted? Also, one of the most beautiful players on the court today is none other than Martina Navratilova, who at forty-five still plays doubles and says she's feeling fitter than she did in her thirties.

Now that it's August, I'm working on my backhand and dreaming of the U.S. Open, the last big tournament of summer. I vaguely hope someone other than Serena will take this one, just for a change. But even if the play is completely predicable, I'll watch every minute.

In the Box Called Pleasure

Kim Addonizio

My husband left me because he felt like he had no power. Now he has it; I call him up and beg him to come over and fuck me. I've just quit cigarettes and all I can think about is how good it would feel to take a deep drag of smoke into my lungs. He pushes his cock down my throat until I gag on it, makes me keep it there until I have to relax; if I don't I'll choke. I relax. Everything is fine between us.

I have papers on my desk that read Dissolution of Marriage. I call and ask my husband for his social security number so I can fill them out; then I scream at him; then I don't do anything. I am having a crisis of self-esteem because I am ugly and stupid, with a bad memory to boot. I forget names, including my own, and most of what happened in books I read. *Madame Bovary,* for example. I remember that Emma kills herself, but not how. *Sentimental Education*: someone named Frederic rides in a carriage and complains and is in love with a married woman. This is in the box called Flaubert. Also: origins of the modern novel. The Seine. Someone making love. A view of mist-covered pines from the apartment I rented one summer. End of box.

After I phone my husband he comes over and mashes

me against the wall with his body. I love the feeling of being physically trapped. It's my worst fear, psychologically, why I ran from all my lovers before him. I realize I've lived by definitions; now there aren't any and it's impossible to function. Nature isn't friendly but it exhibits a profound order. I think that if I could somehow stir myself into it as one more ingredient, I would know how to get through this. He's silent on the other end of the phone and I wonder what he's thinking, if he gives a shit if I live or die. The only way I can get over him is if I die.

I don't die.

I live in a mansion with ghosts. At night the former lady of the house floats, transparent, over the lawn, calling each of her children by name. Sometimes they answer. It's that or cats. A frieze over my fireplace shows a naked man in a chariot, a horse, cherubs, women in filmy robes. I don't touch anything for fear I'll break it. I can't remember how I got here, but it's pleasant enough. The floor shines and there are windows all around, and a piece of furniture called a swooning couch. After a discrete knock, food appears on a tray outside my door; I never see the servants. Mostly I stay in my room, but sometimes I go down the wide red-carpeted staircase and into the drawing room, which is dark and filled with gloomy paintings of people I don't know in elaborate gold frames.

I masturbate constantly, imagining that my husband is ordering me to spread my legs. He slaps my thighs; if I try to close them he slaps them harder. He ties me to the brass bed and I can't get up to answer the servants' knock. After he fucks me he throws a fire ladder out the window, climbs down it and doesn't come back.

I call for help the first few days but nobody comes; nobody even knocks on the door anymore. After a few weeks I starve to death. I rise above my body and it looks so pathetic I can't believe I didn't get rid of it sooner; my mouth is open, my eyes have a scummy film over them, there's shit and piss everywhere, not to mention blood because I got my period. I'm glad my ugly, filthy body can't drag me down any longer; now I'm light as a feather, I spin around near the ceiling feeling like I've just chain-smoked an entire pack of cigarettes. At first it's fun but then I start to get bored with being dead and wonder what else there is to do. I decide to try masturbating and guess what, it's great: when I come I fly into a million pieces and it takes hours to collect myself from the corners of the room. I notice I can't go through walls, though, and that worries me. I don't want to be stuck here in this room with my body forever. It stinks, for one thing. A fly crawls over my cheek and into my mouth.

I'm lonely here, and I miss my husband. I write him a long letter, a letter full of questions about us. What is there between us, I ask him, besides our sex? Is there any point to staying married? What does that mean, anyway? We don't live together. We rarely see each other. I wear my wedding band on my right hand, if I wear it at all. His name is engraved on the inside so I won't forget it. Marriage is *a)* a capitalist institution for the subjugation of women and preservation of male power and authority; *b)* an anachronism; *c)* a way to get health insurance; *d)* a species of insect.

Dear, Darling, Sweetheart:

How I miss your hands on me, the smell of your skin, your tattoos, the harsh tobacco taste of your tongue. Though you should try not to smoke so much. I wish we could talk sometimes, instead of just fucking. You've become a total stranger to me except in bed, where I feel like we're the same person. I know it's the same for you. Marriage didn't kill our desire. Why can't we be friends? Don't you like me, just a little?

Love,
Your Wife

Every day I walk past the table in the hall where the servants leave the mail. There's nothing yet. Long-distance relationships suck. I wish there were someone here to fuck, but I'm too hung up on my husband to even consider it. Most men are lousy fucks anyway; that box is crammed full. Can't get it up, can't keep it up, won't eat pussy, comes in three seconds, holds me like I'm made of glass, can't find my clit, won't use a condom, fucks in total silence, expects me to do all the work, thinks of it as work, as proof of his power, as pure release: I have to come, there's a hole, I'd like to come in that but shit there's a person attached to it. My husband is an incredible fuck. I'm not sure what we do should even be called fucking. How can I give that up?

My husband left me to punish me; I wasn't behaving like A Wife. Fuck that. We didn't know each other very well. I'm starting to enjoy my freedom, even though my heart is a crushed useless lump of tissue that gurgles constantly like bad plumbing. I blame him for everything.

Then I blame myself. Then I blame my father, my brothers, and God. It's impossible to have a relationship, nothing lasts anyway, there are no models, men go into the woods and beat little drums and scream, gender is meaningless, or it's everything; I want a partner, I need to be strong alone since we live and die alone anyway. I want someone to love me. That's what everybody wants, right? Besides being stupid, ugly and amnesiac I am incapable of seeing beyond my own selfish ego. Until I do, I'll never get what I want.

Once we were happy.

Once he looked at me and I knew he loved and wanted me and I wasn't scared he would stop.

Once there was a queen who was the most beautiful woman in the land; everyone said so. Secretly, though, she knew she was a disgusting, hideous creature who had fooled everyone. Either that, or she was totally insane. She didn't know which would be worse, to find out she was really a monster or really a crazy nut, so she ordered her subjects to remove all the mirrors from the kingdom. Her husband the king humored her, but every year on her birthday he tried to give her a mirror as a present, figuring it was a phobia she would overcome in time. Every year the queen refused the present, and ordered the mirror taken out to the forest and smashed with a hammer.

One year the king found such a gorgeously exquisite mirror that the entire court urged the queen to accept it, but it was the same old story: smash the shit out of it. The woodsman whose job it was to do this took it out to the forest, but he couldn't bring himself to ruin such a beautiful object. He went deep into the forest, and there he found a small house where he hid the mirror. He broke a window in the house and brought the pieces back in a leather bag, to prove to the queen that he had done her bidding, and the queen put the bag in the bottom drawer of her dresser with all the other bags from previous years.

One afternoon when she was out jogging, the queen ran farther than she had ever run before, and came upon the little house hidden deep in the forest. Being extremely thirsty, she went inside to look for something to drink. As soon as she entered the house she saw the mirror, leaning against the wall under the broken window. She wanted to leave, but it was too late; as soon as she caught a glimpse of herself she stopped, transfixed, and couldn't look away.

I think all this has something to do with Lacan, whose theories I've forgotten.

Once we were fucking, I was on top, and between one thrust and the next I felt I didn't love him anymore. Suddenly I was just fucking a male body, not his body, and I felt a sense of freedom and power: now I could fuck anyone, do anything, create my own life. Then I was in love with him again and I thought maybe I'd imagined it; can love go in and out like breath?

I've got to find a way to get out of here and get to town. In town there's a store: nail polish. Tampax. Liquor. Cigarettes. Lipstick. I don't have to wait here passively for something to happen. Do you think she saw a monster in the mirror? Makeup, in the seventies, meant slavery to imposed definitions of beauty; now it's assertive, self-adornment, a hip feminist statement.

I hate it that everything changes.

Themes so far: loss of power; loss of memory; self-hatred; definitions. A large crow lands on the lawn. In the box called pleasure:

I'm riding my bike around the streets of our neighborhood. My mom, who happens to be queen of the kingdom, has given me a letter to mail. I'm proud of being chosen to do this, especially since my mom never speaks to me; she spends most of her time shut up in her room, she's beautiful but crazy as a loon. But this morning she called me in, handed me a letter. Her stunning black hair was loose around her shoulders. She used to jog and work out and play tennis, but now she just lies around watching TV all day and she's starting to get fat. I don't think she realizes this because there aren't any mirrors in the house; I have to go over to friends' houses to see what I look like. I'm blonde, I don't look a thing like my mother but I'm cute as hell. I'm six years old and I want to be on TV. My name is Buffie. I adore my mother. When she gives me the letter I feel warm and happy; she hands it to me and kisses me on my forehead.

"Don't tell your brothers," she whispers. "Or your father, either. This will be our little secret. All right, darling?"

When she calls me "darling" I think I'll pass out from being so thrilled. I tuck the letter into a pocket of my dress. She turns back to "One Life to Live," and I go out of her room and down the stairs.

On the second floor I run into one of my seven brothers.

"C'mere, Buffie," he says. "I've got something in my room for you."

My seven brothers are all older than I am. They take me for pizza and ice cream, or ignore me; sometimes they protect me from our violent father, the king, and sometimes they tie me up and torment me.

"What've you got?" I say, suspicious. "I have to go do something for mom."

"It will only take a sec," my brother says.

I follow him into his room. My brother's room is filled with rats: cages and cages of them, sleeping in wood chips or running on treadmills or staring out at me, their tiny hands clawing at the wire mesh. They give me the creeps, like my brother. I don't trust him.

"Sit down there," my brother says, pointing to his bed. He has a can of Pam—spray-on cooking oil—in his right hand. He takes a baggie, sprays the Pam into the baggie, and holds it over my nose and mouth.

"Breathe, Buffie," my brother says.

I take a breath. Immediately my ears start ringing, the room recedes, I know I'm still in it but I'm miles away, I can't find my body. I try to lift my hand, fall backwards on the bed; it takes hours to fall, I keep expecting to feel the bed but don't. I can hear my brother laughing somewhere. Then there's something hot between my legs and I feel like I have to pee, or maybe I am peeing; it's sticky, my underwear is wet, I try to move but I'm trapped under something I can't see. I'm blind. I start to scream; I open my mouth and something cold rushes into my lungs and I feel fantastic, I'm a big balloon, I start to giggle imagining myself as a balloon in a dress, my skin stretched tight over my enormous face I'm laughing so hard now I ache, more cold air filling me up I'm rocking back and forth in a rowboat in the middle of an ocean, rats are swimming by, their hairless tails whipping the water. The boat goes under.

I'm in my brother's room again. My head aches, I'm lying on his bed with my legs twisted open and my underwear off. He's standing over at the wall of cages, his back to me. He takes out a rat and brings it over to the bed.

"Ugh," I say. "Get it away from me." He knows I hate his rats.

"You'd better run," he says, smiling. He makes like he's going to toss the rat at me, but doesn't. I start crying. It hurts between my legs now. I jump up from his bed and run out, leaving my underwear.

I run downstairs to the garage and get on my bicycle. It's a pink five-speed Schwinn with streamers on the handles. As I ride, I feel more wetness come out of me. I press my crotch against the bike seat, rub it back and forth.

At the mailbox on the corner I jump off my bike, then throw myself onto the grass. I lie on my stomach and put my fist under my cunt, between it and the ground, and grind against it. Cars drive by. I can't stop, I hope nobody pulls over. Finally I come. I've never masturbated before this. I don't understand what's just happened.

I remember my mother's letter and find it in my pocket, all wrinkled and creased. I smooth it as well as I can, then open the mailbox and drop the letter into its mouth.

Dear Woodsman:
I hate my husband, the king. Unless you become my lover I'm going to kill myself. I can't divorce him

because I'm terrified to live on my own, without money. If I could look forward to seeing you each week, death wouldn't exert such a powerful pull. I can't live for my children; they're on their own. Meet me at the house in the woods, and bring condoms.

Your Queen

Letters are a woman's form. And diaries. The domestic isn't historical; in most of history women don't exist. The self is constituted in memory, so I don't have a self, just a few ideas for one. I sit for hours in the room that used to be my mother's, looking out at the lawn and the enormous fountain; it's the size of an Olympic swimming pool. I'm dying for a cigarette. I drink too much coffee, chew gum, bite my fingernails; I'm not going to make it. I pull Dante's box out of the closet. Open it a crack, flames and shit and vomit spill out; I've only read the Inferno. My mom's in there. The Geryon flies past my window, or maybe it's an eagle; I should get a bird book. I wonder why birds sing, anyway. Is it necessary for their survival? There's one here that drives me crazy every morning, waking me at dawn. I'd like to sleep in, just once. All night it's ghosts, and then this fucking bird.

Dear Mom,

I don't know what the mail service is like down there but I hope you get this in time for your birthday. Even though you were a lousy mother I loved you; I couldn't help it. I was only ten when you died. Why did you leave me? Why didn't you protect me from my brothers, those shits? My childhood was one long molestation. It's all your fault. How am I supposed to get past this and stop being a victim? Happy Birthday. I'm sorry there's no present but you were always so hard to buy for.

Love,
Buffie

p.s. Would you please stop calling my brothers' names every night? They are all doing fine. They have wives and ex-wives and girlfriends and kids and cocaine habits and big-screen TV's. You're the one that's dead.

I'm so depressed. I try to live as though life has meaning, I know it doesn't mean anything. You get old and sexually undesirable and then you die, or you kill yourself before that. Before my husband left me I felt loved, attractive, sexy: he grabs me by my cunt in the kitchen, leads me to the hall and fucks me on the floor, we're two animals, I love that he never thinks during sex or at least never seems to; I love being the instrument of his pleasure; I love the tiny space on his left eyelid—I think it's his left—where a lash is missing. I can't remember now. I've been abandoned. Or I set things up so he would abandon me; I didn't love him enough, my ex-lovers came out of the woodwork to have lunch and flirt, my husband was jealous, I didn't reassure him. Now I'm suffering.

In that box:

A six-year old boy on his way to school in LA gets caught in the crossfire between two gangs and dies. A man with a Serbian mother and Croatian father gets drafted into both armies, runs away to America; in America he drives a taxi in New York City in summer, a lower circle of hell. In the Wood of Suicides my mother moans. A woman answers an ad for a maid, goes to the door; it's a Hell's Angels house, they pull her inside and rape her, later she escapes out a window and goes home to her alcoholic mother. She's seventeen when all this happens, then finds out she's pregnant and gets an abortion, but it turns out she's carrying twins and the doctor has only aborted one. That night at home she's feverish, delirious, the second fetus comes out, she's hallucinating, passing out; she wakes up, blood all over the sheets. Before this her father fucked her for years; she finally told her mother, who had her committed. She's my best friend.

It is, after all, the love of women that sustains me.

Another friend says, "Do you feel that sex saved your life?" She means boys. Actually I think art saved my life at the time it needed saving, when I was doing too much heroin and fucking junkies and living in roach-filled apartments with gunshots in the street every night and the guy upstairs beating the shit out of his girlfriend. Now art isn't enough; I have that, and friends who love me—they write me letters, even if my husband doesn't—and I'm miserable.

One day I'm whining about my life and a girlfriend looks at me and says, "Well, Buffie, the important thing is to feel bad." She's right, I'm complaining about nothing, I should be grateful.

I'm still miserable.

There's a knock on the door. It's my husband, finally; he's come all this way to see me, he says he's sorry for everything and it doesn't matter what happened between us, whatever it was—who knows what's true or real anyway—he says "I feel the pain and love and desire in your words to me and you're right, darling, sometimes it seems so perfectly simple and natural and right between us, even out of bed on occasion," he pushes me down on the bed, begins to rip my clothes off, *rip* my troubles are over *rip* this is a work of fiction and any resemblance to actual persons can't be helped, *rip rip* my underwear flies across the room, a bird goes up to heaven in a rush of wings and it starts raining, sheets of rain over the lawn and fountain, the roof of the house, the windows are streaming, *rip, rip, rip,* I can't stop remembering love.

I Do

Bill Noble

for Dulce

I want to shape new sounds
from the satin of your skin—
shallis, honnelated, sweence—
to let your breath bell out my belly,
let your tongue-tip dance its minuets.
I want your heart to harp my ribs,
my heart to press your plum-bowl breasts,
my spine to dangle like a necklace
from your lips. Oh, let your seedpearl
whisper secrets we simply cannot keep,
your hips upraise their praise in joining.
Let my honeybear lap soft along your heat
and swim your succor like a smile.
I want your legs to loop my waist,
your arms to hoop my kiss. Like . . . this.
I want to canter camelback,
to saddle-vault and sally—yes, I do.
Come let my seed swing arcs.
Come let me slip and slide you.
Woman, when your eyes roll,
when I lose my spurt of words,
I want our shatter seismic.

I want the rush of mountains
in our arms. I do.
And then to laugh like tasseled bells.
Our eyes are spilling jewels.
Our plainsong throats.
I want. I do. A peace
like horses, running on the hills.
I do. I do.

Fires at Midnight

Brian Peters

So here's the myth: all great sex, all truly vibrant, mind-expanding, shivers-to-the-toes, better-than-porn, memorable-to-the-grave sex is free of relationships. It's the summer in Paris; the beach in Jamaica; the wild abandon of two hours of carnal knowledge in a cheap motel room in Adair, Iowa; the dirty dancing of a one-night stand who wants as desperately not to know your name as you want to fuck like a last request before dying and slip anonymously into the night. That's great sex, the stories say, and the baggage of relationships kills all that.

But that, the Easter Bunny, and the honest lawyer are all figments of your imagination. Nearly all sex is relationship sex, because nearly all sex, and nearly all fantasies about sex, are social constructs. If you think about it, the most constrained, hackneyed, scripted sex on the planet is casual, anonymous sex, because it can only happen among partners rigidly doing What's Expected. Without the time to know a partner, only the safety of "what everyone knows as sex" can really happen, and that's hardly worth fantasizing about.

So what keeps the fire in a relationship?

Listen

Listening is the single sexiest act on the planet, and the basis of all seduction. Being drop-dead gorgeous, having the biggest bank balance in the room, or working your celebrity status will all get you noticed, but they become just another part of the landscape in a hurry. Listening will get you in bed.

At some level you already know this, so let me just remind you where you've seen it. Remember that plain, undistinguished, can't-imagine-why-you-even-try person who sat hanging on every word of that night's object-of-everyone's-desire at a party? The one who seemed to know just the right time to laugh and the right time to touch their arm? The one who went home with them? Remember the been-together-for-years couple who graced dinner with a choreography all their own, each seeming to react almost empathically with the other in their own private dance? The ones that everyone who noticed sighed and said, "Wow, if we could only be like that after all those years? . . ." Listening is how all that happens.

Humans, all of us, give off an unbelievable array of information every living moment—skin temperature, flushed or pale faces, breathing rate, heart rate, set of the shoulders, direction of gaze, smiling, frowning, shaking, steady, and on and on. These aren't identical from one person to another. In fact, if you cross cultures (or sometimes even if you cross the street), you'll find that they are confusingly different. But that's one of the joys of a relationship—you can learn them quite well for people whom you're regularly with.

Happily, the basics are much simpler even than that. You don't have to be Sherlock Holmes summoning up a family biography from scratches on a watch case; it turns out that folks, particularly beloved folks, are willing to tell you straight out—in fact that they're often stumbling-over-themselves eager to do so if they think you really want to know. But that will only happen if you convince them that you really want to hear what they want to say, and set a context where they're comfortable saying it. Most people, for example, respond evasively to questions like, "So sweetheart, what really turns you on in bed?" when headed down the household cleaners aisle in a crowded grocery store.

Sure, really extraordinary listening abilities are the work of a lifetime and a skill to be treasured, but we can at least make a start at it by remembering three things: 1) shut up, 2) don't judge, and 3) care about what your beloved is saying.

Learn

Learning follows from listening, hand in glove, but there's more to it than that. Learning requires being open to that thing we most fearfully want to avoid—that thing that the textbooks and sex manuals blithely call risk. But that's not what scares us. Risk has an upside as well as a downside—the longshot that pays off, the gambit that wins. We're afraid of making mistakes, of looking foolish.

It turns out, though, that hardly anyone learns things worth knowing without making mistakes. Often lots of them. It isn't whether you make mistakes that matters, it's how you deal with them. Make a mistake with anger and denial, and you're simply a jerk. Make a mistake with grace and humor, and you're merely vulnerable. That's among the great joys of a relationship—because being vulnerable is amazingly sexy.

There's still more, of course—you can also learn by studying and creating. I don't mean that you have to consistently come up with ten positions not found in the Kama Sutra before breakfast or anything, just that knowing more about your body, and your partner's body, makes all sex more wonderful. Science has never come close to fully explaining our intricate selves, but it's a good place to start. And time spent in the *Clean Sheets* archives is never wasted.

Lust

Only a true dullard could miss this one—but sometimes we do. All of us are at least a little insecure about our sexuality, and most of us are a lot insecure. Whispering those three little words *I want you* has an amazing effect on our self-esteem, but it takes a lot of listening and learning to do it right. Sadly, a culture of immediacy has left us feeling that when *I want you* isn't followed by our partner tearing off their clothing and humping us like a sex-crazed animal, we've been rejected. How much safer to never say anything so coarse, so often badly timed, so easily misinterpreted.

Say it anyway. Let them know. *I want you* when you're frumpy and disheveled, *I want you* when you're stressed and out of time, *I want you* when you're unapproachably dressed to the nines, *I want you* when you're working, *I want you* when you're sleeping, *I want you* when it's just the two of us together under the stars. So long as *I want you* never means *you're obligated*, lust is a truly healthy thing.

Share

This is the bedrock of all relationships—the sharing. We really do understand that, but we aim too high. We think we haven't really shared unless we've shared the peak experience—the trip we can scarcely afford, the feat we've trained years to master, the event that won't happen again in our lifetimes.

We forget that the little stuff matters. Life is made of moments, the present one being all we have for sure, and sharing them is a pure joy. Sex is made from so many obvious sharings—sharing a hug, sharing a kiss, sharing a bed, sharing our bodies. But there are uncounted other things to share—sharing a sunset, sharing a walk in the rain, sharing an ice-cream cone, sharing a laugh, sharing a tear, sharing our joy, sharing *I want you*. Sharings are additive, somehow. Sharing a sunset brings added meaning to sharing a walk in the rain, and sharing moments of sadness brings an added dimension to sharing moments of joy. And if you wonder about the knowing smile the been-together-for-years couple seem to share, it's just that they know sharing so many moments makes sharing their bodies electric.

Pour Me Out

Kell Brannon

This is what happens when Katie decides I need to "broaden my horizons": we end up in some bizarre place wearing skimpy clothing. True to form, tonight we are standing outside the city's first and only fetish restaurant. It's barely 40 degrees, and we're shivering in our black corsets and tiny, tiny skirts that compromise the respectability of our underthings.

"Katie, the food here had better be great."

"Oh, liven up, Liz! Where's your wild side?" Katie sees herself as a Walt Whitman spirit with an Anais Nin id, and, as such, welcomes new experiences the way a pack of hungry hyenas welcomes a fresh antelope carcass. Not that this is a bad thing, of course; sometimes I envy her sense of adventure, but, being a more cautious type, I wish she'd plan these excursions better. This place is in an alley in a rather poorly lit part of the city, I just saw some creepy-looking characters skulking around and looking dangerous, and, to my knowledge, no one knows where we are tonight.

My sense of adventure, in other words, was at home with a mug of hot tea and some poetry, with a blanket tucked securely around her toes.

The muscled zombie guarding the door gets a nod of confirmation from a bigger, even more muscled zombie who's been checking us over, and he intones "Welcome . . . to SweetMeat," snarling theatrically when he bites off the Ts. I can barely hold back titters. Katie just beams at him, in that wondrous, wide-eyed way of hers. He gives us the low-down on the club; apparently no one is granted Family status until the fifth visit. Ergo, we are not allowed to wear the kicky little studded bracelet that binds us to the clan, and we are thereby restricted from certain privileges, like participating in the stage shows, renting private rooms, or making table reservations.

I steal a glance at Katie, about to ask her if we can just leave, but she is already on her way in. She's been dying to come here for months. Eh, what could it hurt? It's just dinner, after all, I lie to myself.

After we surrender our licenses for the age check (body cavity searches are an extra $25 per person, just inside and to the left, he says), we promise repeatedly to conduct ourselves in a respectful manner, and are at last allowed in. We can feel eyes on us as we shuffle down the candle-lit hall.

"Wow, these must be the private rooms," Katie says; the doors lining the hall are thick, dungeonesque, the kind they put in movies when they want to destroy all hope that the plucky heroes will escape. Each one has a little window cut out, with a sliding privacy panel, controlled from the inside. There are only a few occupied rooms with panels open; the second door on the right contains a naked man suspended by his wrists and ankles, vertically and X-style, with weighted clamps attached to his nipples, a slender rope tied around his scrotum (which looks about to burst), and what looks like dried wax tangled in his chest and pubic hair.

He looks up from his meditation and grins when he

notices us. "Hiya," he warbles.

"How ya doing?" Katie chirps. "Got yourself into a predicament there, I see."

"Nothing too serious. She hasn't even brought out the branding iron yet. She must not be in the mood. Always a bright side, I say."

I'm waiting for him to burst into song when a tiny woman dressed like a fairy, a vision in white gauze and sparkly wings and the curliest blonde hair I have ever seen, pipes "Excuse me!" and shoves past us to open the door. She's got a tray of appetizers. "I got some of those stuffed mushroom caps you like!" With that, she slams the door behind her, which reverberates through the hall, and snaps the little window shut.

Katie keeps on walking like nothing had happened. "Come on! We've got to get good seats for the show!"

"The . . . show? There's a show?" I'm still stunned by the surrealism of a fairy feeding stuffed mushroom caps to a guy with tied-up testicles.

"Yeah, that's the main attraction! A magicienne dominatrix!" I think of disappearing objects and cringe.

"But these . . . I'm not too sure I fit in here, Kate." I glance down and feel my breasts pressing out and up, the cleave between them burgeoning just so; they're just so . . . so visible, and I want to lunge for a menu, slap it protectively over my chest. "I'm a librarian, for Pete's sake!"

"But librarians are the lucky ones who get jumped in porn movies."

"Great. I'm fetish material. I should've brought a big, fat book to carry around. I could offer to slam people's fingers in it."

"Liz, dear. Wine. My treat. Hit the bar."

Ooh. I forget about my breasts. "Done."

It takes us a little while to thread our way in and find an unoccupied spot. The club is crowded, but it's a very civilized mob, orderly and dignified. There is flesh, latex, and metal; we see piercings in more bodyparts than I even thought it possible to pierce. There are groups having a good time, couples or trios engaged in scenarios, and singles scouting for others on the prowl.

We're so busy trying not to gawk that I nearly trip over a large dog, before I realize it's not a dog, it's a man on all fours, sheathed in latex from head to toe, but for a few strategic holes for his face and nether regions. His—his companion? Owner? Whomever he's there with slips him bits of food, which he accepts gently and with grace.

At long last, the bartender hands me a goblet of wine with a knowing grin, and I immediately take a big gulp.

"Check it out! The opening act is starting already!" squeals Katie.

At center stage, a tall, skeletal woman in a bustier and red leather bikini underpants whips a dark-skinned, tied-down woman who, from the sound of it, is obviously a well-trained operatic singer, practicing arpeggios. The wielder smacks the singer with the whip every time she hits the high note, which makes her shriek—"ah-aah-aaah-EYAAAGH!-aah-aah-aaaaah!" The audience claps politely after each set of two or three, providing a smooth opportunity for the singer to catch her breath while the top sucks up the praise.

Katie chats with a young man who has just approached her from the other side, and now leans against the bar next to her. He brushes his open shirt aside to reveal a special belt of some kind, containing four phials of an uncomfortably dark liquid. I lean in just a little, but discreetly, nosey in spite of myself, and catch something like ". . . try a sample first if you wish," at which point he brushes his collar aside, in the same practiced move he'd used with the shirt, exposing a vulnerable spot on his neck. Katie is bending down to eyeball the phials, and I'm about to poke her and hiss something about our mothers telling us never to accept blood from strangers, when I feel a tap on my shoulder. A shortish, skinny man with wild hair, barefoot and in the requisite leather pants, is at my left side. His eyes are startlingly dark, but friendly, with a few weather-lines carved around them. Cute.

"Yes?"

"My wife and I . . . we've got Private Room B. We've been looking for a third, for a long time, and you look like exactly what we've been hoping for."

Great. One guy is trying to sell blood to my best friend, and another is inviting me to hop on in with him and his wife. I haven't even had a date in two and a half months. Unbelievable. "I don't . . . I don't know . . ."

He senses my trepidation and interrupts, waving frantically as if to flutter it away. "It's not like that! You wouldn't be, uh, having relations with either of us. Not exactly," he says with a shy grin.

The tiny ghost of Katie that lives in my cerebellum screeches *Live a little! Live a little!* while it reaches down to fan at the sips of wine I've had already, shooing the buzz prematurely into my bloodstream. And, I must admit, the guy doesn't seem too scary.

To pique my confidence, then, and to shut up the shrill little voice, I try to work up a Sultry Librarian Mode.

"So what would this encounter entail?" I run a finger around the rim of my glass.

"She . . . well, we . . ." He fumbles a little, shuffling his feet, then spits it right out, in a near-whisper so soft I have to lean in to hear it: "We want you to whip her while I watch." I almost drop my wine. "Not hard enough to really hurt her or make her bleed or anything. Just . . .

107

yeah." He shrugs.

Something in his manner is so earnest, so sweet, that my curtain of caution slowly begins to rise. He continues, still emphasizing every phrase with his trademark gestures: "No bodily fluids, no hands-on contact or anything. Just topping her with the whip. She's blindfolded, even."

Katie and the bloodletter are watching us now; they probably couldn't hear his request, but the sense of invitation is, I'm sure, pretty obvious.

"It'll just take a few minutes! You can come right back!" he pleads.

A bubble of once-in-a-lifetime, give-it-a-try wildness rolls up from my belly, swells into my throat, and escapes. "Let's go," I tell him. Katie cackles.

All the way to the room, he explains the deal. They dabble in domination play when they're alone, a little bit of pain here and there, have been together for years, are focusing on fantasies right now. They've been planning this one for a long time. "Her safeword is teapot."

"Teapot?"

"Yeah, teapot."

"As in I'm a Little?"

"Yup."

"She's in the throes of passion and she has to say Teapot when she's ready to stop?!"

"Hey, don't ask me. She picked it out." I'm just impressed with myself for knowing what a safeword is. "Hang back until I get her ready. On my signal, you can start."

"Just start whacking at her? Can I talk to her at all?"

"You've never done this before, have you?"

Geez, am I ever going to yank my foot out of my mouth? Then again, foot-eating might be a fetish unto itself; maybe my subconscious is just trying to get into the scene. "No," I admit, preparing to bolt gratefully if he changes his mind.

He grins again, a wry half-turn at one corner of his mouth. "Neither have we. But that's probably why I picked you. You just . . . don't have the same kind of immersion going on that most of the others here do, so I guess I feel like I can trust you more easily."

"Why not have a friend do this? Somebody you know?"

"She's had this fantasy, like, forever. A stranger is part of the deal." There's a slight downturn in his tone when he says this; I start to ask about it, sensing that he's not completely into the whole stranger-whipping idea either, but we're already there and he shushes me.

When we enter and pull the doom-reckoning door closed, she is in the corner, naked, kneeling serenely with her wrists bound in front of her. She's large-breasted and very curvy, an Earth goddess of a woman, with long, dark hair, worn loose and streaming about her shoulders. The blindfold is woven through it so her waves escape above and below, like the fabric just happened to grow there naturally.

"Carmen, we have arrived. Stand." He says this softly, but with a change in his voice and posturing that makes me jump. He's gone from wild-eyed and twitchy to quiet and controlling; the voice he uses is completely steady, slow, and leaves no smidgen of room for reluctance. She smiles softly and says, "Yes, David," while she slips gracefully to her feet.

He strides over, waits until he knows she is steady, takes some of that lovely hair in one hand, and pulls her head back, just a sharp tug. "As we discussed, Carmen, you will address me appropriately in front of our guest." Again, no room left for question, only absolute obedience, and she replies, "I'm sorry, Sir."

He gently turns her and steers her toward the center of the room, where a short, leather-upholstered bench awaits, with loops at all four corners. "Walk." She does, demurely, and responds to his other brief commands, stop, down, with evenness and absolute calm.

When he finishes buckling her in, she is on her knees and stretched over the bench, hands and feet tied, with her gorgeous, voluptuous ass presented toward the door, where I stand. He's put velvety cushions where her knees and hands touch the floor.

Wordlessly, he pads over, hands me the whip, holds up a single palm as if to say Wait; then he returns and kneels in front of her, close to her head. He gazes down at her and strokes her shoulder fondly; he takes a deep breath, steels himself, then nods and smiles nervously at me.

I smile back. I can't, just can't, screw this up.

So I stalk toward her, letting my boots clack on the floor, hoping they sound a little intimidating, but worried that it sounds like I'm goose-stepping. When I'm close enough to know that she feels me, I trail two fingers up the back of one thigh, along a cheek, and up her spine.

She spasms for several long moments. I can't resist —surely she wants to hear a voice, a feminine voice that will reassure her—so I lean over, close enough to breathe into her ear, and say, in my sultriest, slowest, deepest Librarian Voice ever, "Hello, Lovely."

She emits a yelp, just a tiny one, enough to make me wonder if she's truly scared and almost enough to make me rethink this whole thing before it even starts, but he pulls her head up by a fistful of hair near the crown and scolds, "Carmen, you will keep silent until you are asked to speak."

"Yes, Sir." She calms immediately, and bows her head

again.

If I prolong it much more, the tension will break, so I step away and try the whip out for size, just snap it in the air once; a satisfying crack echoes through the room. I wonder briefly if it's going to hurt like hell, but he's nodding, so I take aim and let fly. Snap—it lands on her back, with flair and a lot of noise, but doesn't appear to faze her. After a couple more tries, successively more powerful, I get a little jump out of her, and instinct tells me to linger in that zone for a bit.

I keep going for a couple of minutes, until she's squirming and breathing heavily. David stops me for a moment and converses quietly, almost silently, with Carmen, holding her face in his two hands; then he gets up, scampers over to me, and whispers, "Can you do it a little harder?"

"Harder?"

"Yeah. Maybe twice as hard."

"But I don't want to hurt her!"

"But she wants to be hurt, a little. Please? I'll let you know if it's too much."

"Oh." Do all dominatrixes fumble like schoolgirls at first? Sheesh. "All right."

He kneels in front of her again, signaling for me to go on. But I've followed him and am trailing the whip's end along her lush curves, noting the faint, reddened marks.

Then I have an idea. I trail the stiff handle of the whip between her thighs, along her soft-furred labia, very lightly. She cries out when it nudges her clit; David nods, enthusiastically, and scolds her again. "Carmen, be silent!" He never raises his voice, but the cold command in it again pokes at something tingly in my belly, and I, too, resolve to keep quiet.

So I resume the whipping, harder this time. Five or

six strokes, and the marks are redder; she's moaning a little now, and he's allowing her to make the sounds, while she strains to reach his groin and mouth him through the leather. He's watching her face, breathing harder; he keeps running his fingers through her hair and over her shoulders and her back, soothing the red spots between smacks. Once or twice he doesn't pull back in time and flinches when the whip bites his fingers; I immediately start to apologize but he shakes his head and beckons for me to keep it coming.

She's moving her ass while I whip her, bucking upward to direct the blows, and I indulge her, letting a few land on the backs of her thighs, pulling ragged moans from her throat. David reaches down and gropes at his side, finds a little rectangular control of some kind, and fumbles with a switch; she immediately tenses and cries out, aloud this time, apparently not caring whether she displeases him; but from the look on his face while he gazes at her, glassy-eyed and with his mouth slightly open, he's anything but displeased right now.

Didn't I just read about a remote-control vibe in a naughty e-zine somewhere? Some writer named after a planet or something, a constellation? But I'm distracting myself. My arm is turning to rubber, so I have to switch the whip to my left hand, but I keep going, though I miss a few before I figure out how to aim correctly with it. I slow the pace dramatically while he fiddles with the control, watching his thumb for cues. Flick—snap! Flick—snap! He flicks it on in the split second before the whip strikes her skin, giving her a surge from within and without, and she rocks back and forth with the power of it.

He's encouraging her. "Come on, sweetheart. Yeah." He's absolutely bulging in those pants, still running his other hand all over her, tangling it in her hair and pulling her deeper into his groin, and she's huffing into it, still doing her best to pleasure him despite the distractions. I can't see the vibe, since it's buried inside her, but I can see the way her thighs tense when she clenches around it, trying to wedge it against her sweet spot without using her hands, as I have done so many times with my own toys, alone in my bed. She writhes to the music of her cunt and she's so wet I can see the light reflecting there, shining down the insides of her legs.

"Please—please!" she breathes, just when I'm not sure I can take any more of this.

"Please what?" The cold, calm voice is back, but his face is soft, smiling down at her, his eyes kind.

"Please . . . let me."

"Let you what, Carmen?"

"Come. I want to come. Sir."

"Okeydokey." He reverts instantly from Master to David; they've both been tortured long enough, I guess. With his free hand he pops the quick-release on one of her hand straps. I expect her to dive straight for her clit, but instead, to my delight, she runs the freed palm slowly up his thigh to squeeze and caress his cock, gnawing at the head slowly with her lips, just for a moment. He holds his breath.

And then she smiles, such a big smile I can see it from behind when she lets her head droop against him, and her hand slides between her legs.

God, this is beautiful.

I almost lose track of my task, watching them, and I start to forget who I am. A stranger, an enabler. A fantasy. Two of her fingers are working inside, pushing the vibe against all the right places; the scent of sex and sweat is everywhere in the room, he's still stroking her shoulders and her hair, and I'm lost in the beauty of it all, of the way he buckled her to the bench earlier, arranging the cushions and tenderly readjusting the straps, gauging the welts carefully, making sure she is safe and absolutely comfortable. I'm lost in the look on his face, the adoration and the trace of fear, the sense that he doesn't really want to share her with a stranger, but he's doing it, just this once, because this, the fantasy, will make her happy.

She keeps rocking, pressing the heel of her hand against her clit, and I keep smacking with the whip, just a few more times. She comes, with long, low screams and so much shuddering I'm surprised the vibe can stay in there. After ten or twelve seconds she gasps, "Teapot, teapoooot! Urrgh!" and I stop.

And then they're both laughing, the shaky, relieved laughter of exhausted afterglow and climbing down. He immediately scrambles to free her from the restraints; she pulls him down, tumbles into him, and they laugh and laugh, arms wound tightly around each other, their cheeks wet with escaping tears. They've completely forgotten that I'm in the room. I'm standing there grinning like an idiot. I think of my safe, girly, pastel-colored vibrator, my lonely apartment, my empty bed that takes forever to warm up when I crawl in, and suddenly I have to blink back a rising flood.

It's time for me to leave them alone. I loop up the whip and lay it down beside them, turning to leave. David has pulled the blindfold off, and Carmen's eyes are incredible, a pale ice-blue that contrasts perfectly with her dark lashes and the peachy-pink, just-came-like-a-wild-woman flush high in her cheeks.

"Thanks," says David, beaming.

"Yes, thank you," adds Carmen. "This was . . . thank you so much."

"No. Thank *you*." I lean in to kiss her gently on the cheek, then him, noting the slightly musky sting of the salt on my lips. And with that, quietly, I leave, though I'm quivery and my legs feel all bockety. On the way out I check the privacy panel, meaning to shut it for them, but it's already closed.

Thank God I drink red wine. I never have to worry about it getting cold.

The magicienne dominatrix has just taken the stage, and her theme music, some kind of sensual techno with chanting in the background, is throbbing through the air and quaking the floor. Katie is alone at the bar now; the purveyor of blood has apparently wandered off in search of other clientele.

My friend takes one look at me and exclaims, "You look like the cat that just ate the canary! What were you doing back there?"

I can't stop thinking about teapots. Handle, spout; tip me up, pour me out.

"Just watching," I tell her. I take a long sip of my wine, waiting for the slow burn to fill me inside, where I feel the most empty.

Let's Roll

Aria Williamson

Everyone tells me not to marry Stephen. *You deserve a whole man,* my mother says, apologetically, over and over again. *He'll never satisfy you, dear,* whispers my aunt who looks like she's never had a good day of sex in her life. *You can love him,* the common wisdom shouts, *but don't crawl into bed every night with someone who can't fuck you right.* There is little for me to say except that he *matters,* and that most days I feel lucky that *he* might want *me.*

How can I tell them about Stephen's hands, just his strong hands, and what he does to me when he touches my arm and trails his fingers down my freckles from shoulder to wrist and back again? How can I describe what it feels like when he knows how to touch that secret spot just inside my elbow, and he circles and circles so gently with just the right pressure until he almost makes me want to come from his touch?

Reader, there are a hundred ways to satisfy a woman, and a smart man in a wheelchair knows them better than anyone else. It is touch and intimacy and attention that women crave. I believe that there is one key thing that both genders long for in their deepest dreams: *to be known.*

To be known: sexually, emotionally, physically. There is a way to touch your tongue to the inside of a woman's thigh that telegraphs *I want you I love you I can't live without you, you're mine and I haven't even touched your clit yet* without ever saying a word. It is a dance of passion, sometimes a silent waltz, often a motionless tango for two lovers who have the exquisite pleasure of living in their own private sensual world.

I will dance with him at my wedding, I tell my well-meaning but closed-minded friends and relatives, *and you will all watch and be happy for me.* My sister says what everyone is thinking— *he can't dance!*—but what do they know? We have danced in my garden; we have danced in bed; we have gone to concerts and I have danced *for him* and *around him* and *on his lap* and he was there with me in every sensation—there are so many ways to hold your lover.

This is what women want, I should tell them: hands and tongues and laughter and sharing and talking—God how we can talk through the night—and a man who knows every inch of your body and who can see right through you and still thinks you're the most extraordinary woman in the world.

Stephen is a brilliant designer; a good pianist; a disciplined weight lifter. Life is just slower and more complex for him—for us—than for others. But he is strong; it is only part of his body that does not function normally, and the part that does is empowered. Me, I can write, it used to be all I could do; now, I can run. He likes to see me run, likes to watch me move the way that he can't. I wear gym shorts and sports bras for him and he times me at the track, and when your love in a wheelchair is your coach and you know he'd do anything to be in your place, there are no excuses for not being better than you ever thought you could be. After running we go home and we shower together, sitting together on his bath seat, soaping each other, and it is childlike and pure yet hotter than any intercourse I have ever had.

We will probably never have children, it's a full-time job just loving each other. We have pets; we have toys—a wicker basket full of ones from Good Vibrations just for us. We've tried it all, but the sexiest thing we do is the simplest. We read to each other. Poems and dirty stories and classy erotica and hard-core pornography, laughing, breathing, sharing, heating each other up. Then when there is no more heat left in us for a while we'll go out someplace and stare down the world, all the people who look at us and wonder why a pretty young woman is with a disabled man, kissing him, always kissing him in public so that no one will mistake her for his nurse.

"Let's roll," Stephen will tell me when he's ready to go home, and it has always meant something special to us, different than what it might mean to the world now, a tiny joke meant to let me know that it's time to get out of wherever we are and go home to our cocoon and love each other through the night.

You have my blessing, my oldest brother finally said to me after 9/11, and we didn't need it, we had our own plan to elope away from all opinions, but instead, as everyone paused to consider meaning and loss and the value of each of our days, we began to plan for a celebration of love and lust and hope neverending, and *everyone* began to dance.

Reader, I married the man.

Long Distance Love Poem

Lawrence Schimel

He cannot see me, but the boy knows
I am writing about him.
If he is asleep, he rolls over without waking,
as if to fold himself into the curve of my body
until we are like two stacked bowls
filled with each other.
As far as the poem is concerned
this is our sole sustenance,
and if we remember brunching
it was only for the pleasure
of feeding one another.

It is six hours later where he is.
When I miss him, I try to imagine how his life
might be, off-kilter from my own.
If it were the morning, he would be at work—
but I write no poems in the morning.
He is probably asleep now and he is
probably alone.

When the poem ends
he will clutch at the blankets,
pull them around himself
because he feels cold.

I will not stop writing.

I, Claudia

Joy James

I find the whole idea of a world championship for
cocksucking incredibly, gloriously erotic. Why not? The
world, at least the Western world, is full of infinite possibilities, and there's equal opportunity for all women,
even me.

Whenever I'm on my knees now (and it's often), I
make believe I'm Claudia. Not Madonna or Britney—
my new heroine and latest role model is Claudia. Her
fame is not due to mere beauty or luck, but is justly
based on merit and perseverance. I believe if I practice a
lot and work hard, just as I'm doing now while kneeling
before a brand new cock, working on my basic bob and
slide, I can become just like her.

Claudia, according to a dispatch from a Romanian
newspaper widely reported on the Web, is the winner
of the first Oral Sex World Championships. Competi-
tors from all over the globe attended the event at a Black
Sea spa. An all-male jury awarded Claudia the $1,000
first-place crown. Their decision was based on "speed"
and "artistic merit" in two rounds titled "technical" and
"freestyle."

At first, when I read this, I chuckled, as most readers did, I'm sure. But, ever since, I haven't been able
to get it out of my pretty, come-sucking head—a head

no longer chuckling, but giggling and giddy. I'm jealous! Like Claudia, I want to be internationally recognized for my abilities (at least all the guys tell me I'm able)!

The purity of it all excites me: cock sucking for the sake of cock sucking, in and of itself, having absolutely nothing to do with love or any other emotion that might get in the way of technique and performance. But think about the bonding going on between the cock sucking performer, the anonymous owner of the succulent cock, and the observing audience! It's one of those once-in-a-lifetime, life-altering experiences when minds, not just bodies, truly connect. It makes my mouth water just thinking about it. The idea of it alone is enough. I can't think of a better expression of eroticism.

I want to be Claudia! The epiphany pops into my head at the exact moment when I'm licking the underside shaft of my latest prize of a penis. Or if not Claudia, at least second-place finisher, shedding genuine tears of happiness for the winning girl. Instead of a crown, I could then wear a tight T-shirt, with my hard nipples poking the fabric, flaunting the fact: "Miss Fellatio World. First Runner-up." The mind boggles with all the fresh cock I would attract.

My lover has no idea what's going through my head as I'm giving head. That's part of the fun of it; I remain a mystery to him. He, on the other hand, is totally exposed, vulnerable to my every tongue-flickering whim. I know exactly what he's thinking; he tells me so. Even taciturn men feel compelled to talk to me when my mouth is full. While I'm sucking like a vacuum cleaner, they are spitting out appreciative, flattering words:

"Look up at me while you're sucking, bitch. I want to see your gorgeous, fluttering lashes and grateful, smiling eyes while your sexy lips are around my cock."

They ask questions: "You like to suck cock, don't you? You're just a cock-sucking cunt, aren't you? Tell me, cunt, isn't this the best cock you've ever tasted? You can't get enough of my fat, juicy cock, can you? You don't want to ever stop sucking, do you, bitch?"

Of course, I can only answer with my head—a vigorous nod or a swaying shake. Those well-executed head motions just add to the cock owner's pleasure. And it is his pleasure, after all, that brings me mine.

Actually, what I want him to tell me is how I'm doing—a real critical review. Vague praise is meaningless: "This is the best blow job ever . . . slut, you suck so fine . . ." Blah, blah, blah. I've heard it all before. What I crave—besides cock, of course—is brutal honesty. And the more detailed the critique, the better.

Unfortunately, most suckees are hopeless in this regard. All they care about is "shooting me a pearl necklace" or whether or not I'll "swallow." They're so ecstatic just to get a blow job, they don't really notice, much less appreciate, my truly expert level of keenly honed presentation.

Do they consider the pronounced, feminine arc of my back and butt while kneeling (evolutionary biologists call this "the fertility curve")? Can they award points for the dexterous way my hand moves at the base of the shaft, so it's synchronized with all my various mouth actions at the most sensitive tip? Are they connoisseurs of how even the eloquent (dainty, yet firm) grip of my hand ensures that my finely French-manicured nails are showing? Are they closely observing the vigorous, quick tempo of my acrobatic tongue, lip, and neck movements, as calorie-burning as my aerobics class—without my face working up even one tiny bead of perspiration, much less ruining my makeup (except my lipstick, of course)?

True, Olympic-level cocksucking is just like ballet. Unless you have actually executed a perfect pirouette on point while dressed in tights and tutu, even the most avid dance-goer hasn't the foggiest notion of how hard it is to make it look so easy.

What would Claudia do? I figured it out that she probably has her very own professional coach. I decide to confess my need for Olympic training to the owner of one of my all-time favorite, most suckable cocks. He always brags about how many "wenches" have given him head, so I can learn from his critical comparisons and contrasts. But he quickly counter-proposes with what he calls "a better idea." He'll set up a School for Sluts. I'll teach Cock Sucking 101, for which his cock will be my students' teaching aid. Clearly, he has his own fantasy.

Like most heterosexual men, he just doesn't get the point. This is not fantasy for me; it is a clearly defined mission, with a measurable, achievable goal: to be Claudia, to reach beyond my grasp of the cock I now have in my mouth, to attain the world acclaim that I know can be deservedly mine. The men I suck must remain really no more than props, and I'll use them as such.

As if I'm on a diet, I make a vow: to ingest several different cocks daily. Variety is important, for you can never tell what shapes and sizes the judges will poke at you. I set up a video camera in my bedroom, to tape each encounter. My trial subjects don't mind; I make a copy for them; my mouth is the gift that keeps on giving, and they now have a free porno movie to watch whenever they're horny and lonely.

Style, agility, poise. These are the qualities that my—immortalized on video—cocksucking images help me to develop. No longer do I have to replay my head action in memory. I confess, watching my mouthful-of-cock self on the VCR is quite a turn-on. But I force my brain to maintain laser-like focus on my quest—perfecting my cock-sucking performance.

Which raises a fundamental question: are the contest judges what the New Journalism termed "participant-observers," or do they simply sit back and witness? It makes a great deal of difference in how I orchestrate my cock sucking. What's visually pleasing is not necessarily the most instantly pleasurable sensation for the suckee. So I seek some splendid compromise, trying to score the highest points in both categories—visual and tactile.

Just like this is a Miss America competition, the one single thing I must constantly remember—so that it becomes an involuntary reflex like gagging—is the importance of smiling while sucking. First, you must smile for the camera, judges, and audience, as every girl is taught from an early age to make herself pretty and pleasing to others. Second, of course, you're smiling specially for the suckee, so that he knows you know you're extremely lucky to be blessed with his unique cock in your mouth. Plus, from a purely physiological point of view, it's pleasantly surprising how the facial muscles used in smiling bring added pleasure to the cock. Finally, to be able to maintain that happy expression while an eight-inch cock is being thrust deep down your oral cavity relaxes the throat and mitigates the gagging. I can see Claudia smiling now, as I breathe deeply through my nose, relax my throat, and swallow an enormous brand-new cock. Visualization: that's key in any athletic training.

I'll wipe the smile off Claudia's face when she sees my second-come routine. This is my specialty. Just about anyone with a mouth can make a cock come. But only an expert mouth like mine can create, just minutes later, a second come shot from the very same, formerly flaccid, cock.

A real competitor doesn't discount the importance of costume, either. Normally, I prefer a snug, sexy micro-mini, exposing my panties when I kneel, together with an extremely low-cut top, so that he can shoot it down my cleavage if he wants. That's what I'll wear for the contest, I assume. Or maybe the competition will feature both swimsuits and evening gowns, in which case I'll pack, respectively, my multicolored string bikini (whose top I'll shed when I perform) and my creamy Versace knockoff. The eroticism of the latter I find particularly appealing, mixing high fashion with the lowest, hard-core porn.

For the freestyle event, if the judges allow a costume change, my plan is to don an all-black catsuit, together with a mask like S/M people use. The mask will have a huge hole for my mouth, plus tiny, imperceptible slits for my nostrils, so I can breathe when my mouth is full. I don't even need holes for my eyes; I can see with my mouth. The point here is to present myself simply as a femininely curved, well-toned body with nothing but a come-hole for a mouth.

I bet Claudia hasn't even thought of that: to present oneself simply as a mouth for cock like the famous old "glory hole" of gay-cruising public bathrooms. There shouldn't be any decorative distractions, not even earrings, when I lie on my back on the gymnast's horse—my head tilted upside down over the edge to deep-throat the longest, thickest dong with which the judges want to test me. The more you can level out the bend in your neck, the more your throat can act just like a cunt. That's one of the nuggets of wisdom you gain only through sucking.

Then, in the same position, I'll take two cocks at

once. So I must remember to ask my dentist for one of those oral surgery clamps to practice stretching my mouth. Also I'll need lots more collagen shots for my pouty, bee-stung lips, to make them just like a cunt.

A related routine I want to perfect is simultaneously playing a number of cocks like a xylophone. At the World Championships I'll have a row of men, maybe ten, lined up on the stage. The trick will be to make them all come at almost exactly the same time. This requires unusual patience and perception on my part, which I'm confident the judges will recognize. When I start to taste the pre-come from one cock, I'll have to move immediately to the next, and so forth, and then back again.

I'll need more than a few good men to help me practice this event. So if you want to help my most girly, Cinderella-like dream come true, do be a Prince Charming, won't you, and volunteer! We'll make Claudia incredibly, lustfully jealous with my nonstop practicing to take her crown. Although this provides a wonderful excuse to service my insatiable oral needs with countless numbers of men, still, my pretty, come-sucking head remains full of worry:

What will I say during the contest's interview segment? This has to be part of the contest's new format and it's as anxiety-producing as how I'll style my hair that championship day. What will Claudia and the other girls say? What will I say when the moderator asks me the question: "How would you make the world a better place?"

Media Frenzy

Diana Cage

Digging through the stack of magazines by my girl-friend's bed, mostly *Details* and *Sports Illustrated,* with some *Vanity Fairs* and a few motorcycle magazines, I find a copy of *Hustler.* Two years old, the cover a little bent, but the girls look the same as if they were printed today; glistening with oil, or maybe sweat. Their breasts jut straight out, varnished and hard like holiday hams. Their cunts have tiny tufts of pubic hair that point the way to the carnation pink insides, tinted in Photoshop by an art assistant who probably pinkens hundreds of pussies a month.

There'd be no reason for Anne to hide it from me. She knows I love porn, the skankier the better. I'm sure it was just coincidentally shoved towards the bottom of the pile. But I've never seen a magazine like this one in her house. She never buys the stuff, not even *Playboy.* She claims to hate straight porn. Can't stomach all that cock, or the long-nailed skinny girls, she says. When I talk about images that get me hot—girls tied up, sub-missive, debased, begging for it—she reminds me that she has feminist sensibilities and the look she gives me makes me embarrassed by my traitorous libido.

I wonder if she jerks off while looking at these pic-tures. Suddenly I realize that in the year we've been together, I've never once seen her jerk off. I've prodded myself with every toy she owns as well as a few juicy-looking kitchen implements. Pranced around her studio apartment naked save for a butt plug in my ass and clamps on my nipples. All for her enjoyment. But she has never once reciprocated. I'm a voyeur, she says.

How does she do it? Does she use a vibrator? Does she even take off her pants? I picture her thick fingers parting her bush, finding her hard clit. The fingers at the end of her well-muscled arms. The same fingers that feel so good in my cunt. The fingers that she uses to tease my pussy open before her fist—jammed against my cervix —reduces me to a panting, mewing, begging hole. Those fingers.

Small hard circles, she tells me when I touch her. As if I would try anything else. I love it when she tenses up, her clit a hard knot beneath my tongue, her fist clutching a handful of my hair, shoving my face into her wetness until I can't breathe. She holds me there and I had better hope I took a big breath before she started to go off—because there will be no more air until she finishes.

The thought of her looking at these pictures, jeans pushed down, fingers dipping into wet, salty pink, making circles, furtively putting in a digit or two and then banging herself silly, oh god, it makes me wet. I clench my thighs together and concentrate on the heat in my crotch as I turn the pages. I wonder which spread does it for her the most? I bet it's the voluptuous black chick with the retro hairdo getting the all-anal action. Yeah, that's the one all right. The model's pretty face gives a mixed message. Is she saying "Fuck me harder" or "Get that thing out of my ass"? Your choice.

The image is too much, and my throbbing clit demands attention. I push my skirt up, *Hustler* girls for-gotten; in my mind Anne is on her back. Her jeans and jockey shorts are bunched around her boots. Her tanned skin is clammy, she's breathing hard. Her work shirt is open and she's wearing clamps on her small hard nipples. Her crew-cut hair is damp with sweat. She's jamming two fingers into her cunt and rubbing her clit at the same time. Her face is red, and all her muscles are tensed. She swears under her breath *fuckfuckfuckfuck* as her fingers push her closer to orgasm. She groans and it sounds like a growl.

Oh baby, let yourself go, I think. Let it come. I push my panties to the side and softly touch my own pussy. I'm slick with excitement. My fingers move quickly and lightly over my lips, spreading the wetness. My clit is a hard button, a marble. I roll it between my fingers. The excitement climbs up my cunt into my breasts and arms and hands. I'm on fire. Everything—pussy, ass, clit, fingers—united into one ball of tight heat.

I lean back into the pillows and go to town on my aching clit. My fantasy Anne is breathing hard. She's moaning loudly. I flip her over. She's on her knees taking it like a faggot from some unseen top. She's yelling her head off, bucking against a hard cock, demanding it *harder, faster, more*. In real life, Anne comes quietly. She grunts softly and jerks her body off the bed. I'm the screamer. Sometimes she fucks me so hard that I'm hoarse the next day.

My orgasm is quick and salty, like fast food. I come with a mixture of pleasure and guilt. Panties back in place, skirt down, the blush on my chest and neck begins to fade. Does Anne know what I just did to her? Should I mention that I found her secret stash? I humbly close the magazine and stick it back into the middle of the pile, right where it was before, nestled snugly between Johnny Depp and Michael Jordan.

the bones want to fly

Mary Anne Mohanraj

for Kevin

when you are old
your skin will be delicate
   fragile as tissue paper
my breath will rustle against it
my fingers will slip over the folds
   under the creases
   slide into the secret places
      (I am always discovering
      new secrets within you)
the bones beneath that skin
   will be light bird-bones
they will want to go up
   want to fly sunward
      they will glow through
      the skin, at night, when we lie
      beneath the covers
it is too warm here
you will cry
I am burning up
   I will coax you to stay
   I will lick sweat from your pale neck
   and blow on that shivering skin

I will lick my way down
  (I have done this so many
  many times already)
I will lick circles on your sunken chest
I will lick all the way down, and take you
entirely inside my mouth
until you lose yourself
until you are no longer bound
by earth and skin and bone
  (I have done this, and will
  a thousand thousand times . . .)
afterwards
I fall asleep
  my head resting on your stomach
  one fragile arm flung over
  your thin thigh, and hip
  (it is not much to hold you down)
you will lie there in the dark
  hand buried in my silvered hair
  listening to the wind
    flying
  through the trees

Lube the World, I Want To Get Off

Alex M. Quinlan

A crowd of naked people running around the house for the weekend—getting acquainted, getting intimate, getting off—that's the kind of party my friend Joan, and her husband John, were planning when they consulted me as their sex-party expert. We knew we needed a Friday night icebreaker—something a little more interesting than Lewd Scrabble or Naked Twister.

The old Mazola parties of the eighties came to mind, with the image of a small room, lots of oil on the floor, and hot sweaty people seeking even hotter sex. But these days we know that Mazola (or any other real oil) isn't latex-friendly, and not quite slick enough for the deeply satisfying games we were looking forward to. Not willing to give up easily, I researched, remembering a friend who had bragged about finding a powdered lube ideal for fisting women.

We found it, we ordered it, and we got ready to play. Fed-Ex delivered a two quart jar of a powder called J-lube, which, when mixed with water, formed this amazing slippery substance that bore a great resemblance to the juices that come from a woman who's been orgasming. (The product is meant to be used by veterinarians, so we played quite doctor-like while ordering.)

When I arrived at the party, I found some unusual sex toys next to the door: half a dozen water guns of varying sizes and a ten quart pot covered in clear plastic wrap, with an odd, viscous fluid in it. Inside a smaller room were three barefoot people armed with duct-tape, fastening an enormous plastic tarp to the walls. They'd managed to find one that had no seams and was large enough to cover the floor of the 8 x 10 room and reach about halfway up the walls, to protect the carpet.

Hours later, after dinner and laughing through the vet catalog that we had received with the lube—"Instant Branding!" "Is Your Goat Too Aggressive? Use the Elastrator!"—a pile of nervous, giggling people, including yours truly, stripped naked outside the door and went inside to sit on the plastic-wrapped floor. The uncovered pot of lube and the filled water-guns were handed in to us by the audience of folks too timid to join us, who sat outside in the larger room eating popcorn and listening to music.

We discovered, after splashing around, that the floor of the room was somewhat off-level. This meant two things—all the lube eventually flowed to one corner, and then, all the people did too. This created a new game: Spin The Naked Person. Someone would sit cross-legged, and a number of folks would grab hold of their legs—or anything that we could get a not-so-slippery grip on—and start to spin them. Once we let go, they would bounce off a couple of walls, spinning across the lubed floor. Invariably they ended up in the same corner as most of the lube, with a resounding splash.

Sex was in the air, but it was still funny just to watch people try to move around. No matter what sort of motion they tried to use, they would always slide back, often slipping all the way down into the lube. This was especially amusing when the people were trying to leave the room ("no, no! it won't let you go!"), and when new people who had arrived after we started to play tried to join in—like my long-distance lover, who had driven sixteen hours to see me and join in the party.

Joan slid over to me as I sat happily in the lube and laid her hand on my knee. "May I touch you?" she asked, obedient to the consent-rules of the party. Tall and pale, with auburn hair and cuppable breasts, her hazel eyes seemed to be challenging me. I suddenly flashed on some of her previous behavior, and the light dawned—she had been flirting with me, and I had been too dense to notice. "Sure," I said, as I had noticed a long time ago that she was quite delicious. We quickly ended up with her between my outspread legs, facing away from me.

Never one to pass up an opportunity, I started fondling Joan's nipples. "I don't understand what it is that I had to consent to," I said with a wicked grin. In response, she started to tickle me, but I am not ticklish. She, however, was ticklish, and I made use of this, sliding my fingers into all sorts of places as I wiggled them. The people on either side of me—my long-distance lover, broad and strong, who I hadn't seen in months, the other a complete stranger who was dark-haired and tall with very large hands—braced me against the wall while I reached for every spot on her body that was suggested by the audience.

I found out that her breasts were not ticklish, and neither were the joints of her hips, her lush ass, nor her inner thighs. With the aid of the lube that was all over everything, she could slide out of any grasp I could get on her body, resulting in me fondling every solid, warm, slippery inch of her in my quest for ticklish areas. The folks who weren't involved in holding me stable against the wall made sure to keep us well slicked, showering us with puns and dubious advice along with water from their squirt guns.

Somehow she turned the tables on me—she managed to get herself out of my grip and turned around to face me. She dove her hand between my legs, stroking and probing. I was startled, frozen by the sudden realization of her serious sexual interest.

My body soon took over, responding to her insistent fingers, and to the erotic feeling of being restrained against the wall. She worked her hand in my crotch, scooping lube from the floor, sliding along my labia, then more and more inside me. I'm an easy orgasm, to my everlasting relief, and she was rewarded with wave after wave of my shuddering release from just the fingering. This was mixed, however, with my body uncontrollably flinching and pulling away as she pushed harder and further inside me, until I finally realized she was trying to fist me.

"It won't work at this angle!" I gasped out between spasms, caught in the feedback loop that my body creates. It didn't stop her from trying, crouched between my outspread legs. My lover started pinching my nipples, and the stranger on the other side kept me pinned with his large hands holding me upright.

I don't know how long this continued, but the crowd had finally thinned down to eight people—a different eight than I remembered, as more people had arrived at the party and joined us in the room while I was on my orgasm-coaster, some driven away by my screams and some attracted—when she pulled her hand back and said, "Okay, lay her down."

I was dazed as my body was moved, pulled away from the wall with unknown hands sliding over my skin and laid down on my back, my head resting in my lover's lap. The stranger who had been holding my other side scooted down also, lying next to me and starting to suck on one nipple while another person I didn't know laid himself between me and the wall and sucked on my other nipple.

Joan knelt between my legs and scooped lube from the corner, liberally coating her hand. Sliding her fingers easily into me again, she worked her hand forward and back, in and out, as I whispered to her about what worked and what didn't. I'm used to getting fisted, but any sort of pinching would pull me right out of the delicious delirium, so I was telling her things like a squeaked "Not there!!" and groaning "turn it, turn it, yes that's it" until she finally twisted her wrist the last right way and it popped into place.

My eyes flew open and I shuddered all over when her hand slid into place. I saw a lover of hers kneeling behind her with his body rocking slowly, one hand on her leg and the other invisible. His eyes were hot on me, licking his lips, as whatever he was doing to her made her lift her body and gasp. Her breath was shaky and her voice randomly squeaked when she started shifting and twisting her hand inside me, learning the motions that would make me come with just a twitch.

There was music serenading us. When someone put on Heart's "Dreamboat Annie" CD, everyone was startled to hear me singing along. Even when I was panting for breath, apparently, my lips kept singing the lyrics of the songs engraved so deeply in my mind. I remember waves of orgasms rolling over me as Joan's hand moved in and out, up and down, stroking all of my insides with her fingertips.

After a long time of multiple orgasms, she slowly worked her hand free with a pop, and sat back. "Gee, it really does feel like a nose," was her first comment, and she giggled at the roomful of confused faces looking back at her. "The cervix," Joan explained, grinning at me.

"Yours, in fact."

For some reason this was incredibly funny, and I finally lost control completely, whooping in laughter as she and her lover crawled out of the "Slime Pit" to clean up. As I calmed down, I found my lover nibbling on me —well, trying to bite me, really, as he frequently bites my shoulder as an erotic act. But my skin was so slippery that he couldn't even manage to bite. He grinned at me and sat up with his back to the wall, saying "My turn. It's been four months. Too long."

There was a small basket of condoms in the room for people to use, and my lover picked one out of the pile —or tried to. His hands were too slick to grab just one. With help, he got it in hand, but then found that he could not open it. The people in the room all tried to help, but whether or not their hands would have kept a grip, all were laughing too hard to be able to pry open the small slick plastic package.

Joan poked her head back in, careful not to get caught in the lube, to find out what was so hysterical. Seeing the problem, she handed in a different brand of condom, one that came in a hard gold foil shell, which we could open. But it got fumbled into a puddle of lube, which made it impossible to put on, by him or by me. We eventually had to coax Joan in again to help with her clean hands. She brought with her three more condoms, and after much effort they got a condom onto his cock. He clambered over me to fuck me at last, and as soon as he leaned on me, I squirted out from under him like a watermelon seed.

Over and over again I slid away. No matter what position we tried, it was impossible for me to stay on him or him to stay on me. After ten minutes of vaude-ville-level pratfalls, we finally insisted that the onlookers give us a hand. They braced themselves, seated, against one long wall. They put their feet against my shoulders, holding me from moving across the floor, and my lover mounted me with his feet braced against the other wall. At long last we achieved penetration.

Only I was laughing too hard to orgasm, hard enough that my lover was having a difficult time staying inside me. Our helpers didn't help, being involved with such commentary as "Captain, I canna hold her anymore, she is slipping away from me!" and "Scotty, do yer best!" and "She's breaking up, she's breaking up!", and a rousing rendition of the chorus to the Paul Simon song "Slip Sliding Away."

Eventually we finished, and felt the need to finally clean up. The larger outside room was empty, except for Joan, who was being vigorously fucked by her lover. They didn't notice our emergence, as her voice spiraled up in her distinctive orgasmic cries, loud enough to drown out any noises we had been making. We sat quietly, passing around a towel to scrape off as much of our lube as possible, until the pair of them were done. Their passion was nearly enough to wake my body again, even after all the orgasms I had already had, and I led the enthusiastic applause.

Making our way into the hot-tub area, we found a couple whom I didn't know. They had been in the room with us, and they thanked me for being so uninhibited and inspiring. Apparently they had been fucking in a corner and I had never noticed. I thanked them. I was beyond blushing at that point, and I joined my lover and Joan and her lover in the communal shower.

I've never laughed so hard in my life while having sex. Even now, years later, I remember those five hours first before other, more intense and romantically meaningful events that happened later the same weekend.

At the Wane of the Moon

Bill Noble

When just the sliver of a moon was climbing through the oaks, Beth came home with a story to tell. She shed her thick crocheted sweater, slipped out of the old flowered dress, and draped her clothes helter-skelter over the bedside chair. She slid under the covers, pale as a wraith, to breathe a single word.

"Tom."

Tom turned his face toward the slanting moonlight with an affectionate murmur. He kissed her papery fingers and withered cheek.

"Tom." She brushed his temple with her cool lips.

"Is everything all right?" He opened his eyes suddenly.

"Oh, yes," she whispered, "oh, yes."

She kissed his eyes shut again and pressed herself against his frailness. She slipped a hand over his belly to cup the bony crest of his hip. "I came down the canyon from my evening walk. It's such a warm night. I came down by Jason's. I . . . I watched Jason and Bianca make love. I sat on the hill for a long time, watching them."

" . . . the grandchildren?" His eyes fluttered open again.

"The curtains were open. I came down through the

woods past their house. I could see candles burning, and then Bianca walked in front of the window, just shining. You know, her breasts were so lovely in the candle glow, and Jason caught her up from behind and kissed her."

"*Elizabeth*," he said. He always called her that when he disapproved of something. She laid a finger across his lips to shush him.

"Thomas," she teased. "They were beautiful, and it stirred me, so I watched. At my age I can watch if I want." He heard the determination in her voice, and knew better than to argue.

She kissed along his collarbone, then let her mouth rest for a while over the pulse at the side of his neck. He sighed and she began to stroke his chest and belly, tenderly and slowly. "We have such a sturdy grandson," she said. "He's such a wonderful father and such a dear of a husband. I knew right off the two of them would make a good pair." She traced fingertip circles around Tom's nipples until he sighed again and shifted closer against her. "I have to say, when he picked her up like that—oh, the way she looked at him after they kissed, Tom! But when he stood there with her in his arms like that, so strong and easy, and her perfect round bottom—well, I have to admit, I blushed a little. I almost looked away when his penis was bobbing around like that, right under her . . ."

"Elizabeth," he said again, but she bent forward and put her lips over his nipple. Then she raised her head to look him in the eye. She gave him a peculiar little twinkle, kissed him on the nose, and disappeared under the covers. He sighed. "Beth, it must be terribly late. We need to sleep."

"Can you hear me all right down here?"

"Yes, Beth, but . . ."

"Then just listen. I want to tell you about it."

"Beth, I don't think . . ."

She began to brush her cheek and lips gently against his penis. "Well he just stood there with her in his arms, right beside the bed. They kissed a bunch more—oh, for a long time—and then he began to lick her breast —you know, great, long strokes with the whole flat of his tongue, just the way I used to like you to lick my breasts. And his penis jumped every time he licked her. You know, it's curved up as if it was trying to look around, just like yours. But, oh, Tom, she has the loveliest breasts. Were mine ever so beautiful, do you think, when I was twenty-eight?"

He began to stroke her back with his fingertips. He reached a hand to cradle the furrowed scar on her chest. A tear trailed down his cheek onto the pillow.

"Well, Bianca reached down and grabbed hold of Jason and started to stroke him. Like this." She began a slow up-and-down with Tom's still-sleeping penis. "You should have seen the way his legs locked up and his butt clenched! Your grandson's a real stallion, Tom Maynard. He takes after his grampa."

"Anyhow, Jason dumped her right on the bed. Then he threw her legs up over those big Maynard shoulders of his and just buried his face in her. She made the most amazing noise—I wouldn't know what to call it. Right through those double-paned windows and all."

"Beth, really . . ."

"Well, really, your old proper self! You remember the things we used to do? Remember the time you took me skinny-dipping way up Slater Brook, and by the time we were through we could only find enough clothes lying around for one of us to get home with? I had to go in your pants and fetch you back another pair. Or the time we spent the weekend at the Brenners' and never got up till noon—oh, I'm sure we must have been forty then—and Dewey and Jill blushed all the way through lunch, and hardly spoke? Oh, Tom, we were a pair, weren't we?" She slipped her lips over the head of his penis and began to waltz little circles with her tongue. After a few minutes of silence, she took her mouth away to ask, "Does this still feel as good as you always used to tell me it did?"

"You never would take no for an answer, would you?" Tom laughed. A muffled chuckle came back from under the covers, and for some reason it was the chuckle that seemed to set him stiffening. He was torn between surprise and a sudden onset of delight.

Beth began to slurp and suck, waggling her face, clowning over him. Another laugh welled up, and he felt Beth's stomach begin to shake in silent accompaniment. He grew fully erect.

Beth wet her hands and stroked him vigorously. "Should I tell you what Bianca's climax was like?" He started to say something, but she continued, "It didn't take her long. Tom Maynard, you're as hard as a prize salami. I do believe you're enjoying this!

"Anyhow, she just kept making those noises, but she started to shake, bouncing around on the bed. Jason had to wrap his arms round both her legs to hold her in place. I was afraid the poor boy was going to break a tooth trying to keep his mouth on her!" Tom reached between Beth's legs to pet her. She squealed a girlish little squeal and then lifted one leg to straddle him. He caught her rich humusy smell and felt the fullness and heat of her engorgement. She stroked him hard and fast, then slowed to an almost painful delicacy. He felt the warmth of her lips on him again for a moment before she reverted to full hard stroking with her hands.

"Bianca left big red welts all down his back. And she threw her head back so far I was afraid she was going to break her neck. I'm surprised you didn't hear the commotion all the way over here. Her shaking just went on and on and on. You should have seen the way Jason was thrusting against the edge of the bed—but he never took his mouth off her. Shall I tell you what happened next, what Jason did?"

"Wait, Beth, wait."

"You want me to stop?" She was prepared to be outraged.

"No, no. Mercy, just for a minute. I want to do something." He sat up on the edge of the bed, trying to catch his breath. Beth had emerged from the covers and was watching him quizzically. After a moment he turned on the little bedside lamp and hobbled to the dresser. He rummaged through the bottom drawer and returned to the bed.

"What have you got, you mischievous man?"

Deadpan, he handed her a tube of lubricant. She grinned up at him.

"Tom Maynard, I believe I've had an effect on you! But what are you hiding behind your back?"

He laid a faded photograph on the sheets. She took him in her hand and stroked him toward hardness again, turning to look at the picture. "Tom! I didn't know you kept these!" The photo showed two strong young bodies coupling on a lawn next to a stately bed of iris. The picture was slightly askew. The tops of the couple's heads were cut off. "Oh, Tom! Do you remember how the camera kept falling down every time the shutter went off? And how hard it was to run back around and try to get inside me again before the thing fired? Oh, I didn't know you still had these! Do you remember," she laughed, "we had to find an ad in some sleazy magazine and mail the film all the way to Chicago?"

"You're a beautiful woman, Elizabeth Ann Maynard." He laid her down on the covers. He put a pillow on the floor to cushion his stiff knees and knelt between her legs. "It's my turn."

She held the picture, gazing alternately at it and at the disheveled snowy hair and familiar old head that pleasured her. She couldn't name the reason for the tears they brought. She tried to continue the story of Jason and Bianca, to give Tom something of the wonderful images that moved in her mind, of the run of the muscles in Jason's haunches and down the length of his candlelit back, but the words trailed away unresolved. Her sounds, when she came to them, long after words had failed, told a story they both seemed to know well.

He moistened her with great tenderness, inside and out, and she lubricated him and brought him quickly to erection again, smiling. He entered her with a long, moaning exhalation while she held his face between her hands like an unexpected prize. They kissed in lazy delirium, first one moving, and then the other. They anticipated one another's pleasure, knew when to give respite, when to take up the rhythm again. When he climaxed, her hands clutched his buttocks, pulling him deep into her. He held himself carefully inside long after they were through.

After a time, Tom turned out the lamp. She helped him lie beside her, side by side as the moon receded across the bedroom floor. Long after it had vanished they turned and moved into one another's arms, breath and pulse flowing together, one indistinguishable music in the deepening night.

The General's Dream

Jennie Orvino

What if the compulsion to war
was really a longing to be touched—
to forfeit vengeance
by teasing a nipple to hardness
to find righteousness
in a woman's orgasmic cry?

Pick Me Up Cocktail

Shanna Germain

It's another slow night at the bar—five or six of the regulars sitting at the countertop, smoking more than drinking, and a couple of couples making doe eyes at each other over the cocktail tables. I'm about to give my manager the "It's totally dead" speech—to see if he'll let me go home early—when I see her walk in. That long, straight hair you think only exists in those stupid hair-care commercials, and bare legs beneath a black mini-skirt. A T-shirt cut down to there, low enough to make all the old men at the bar sit up straighter in their chairs and wipe a hand through their thinning hair.

I give a sigh, knowing I'm going to have to ID this chick, and then debate whether to throw her out when she shows a fakey. On one hand, I've got my butt (and my job) to save. On the other, a hot chick in the bar means the regular penny-pinchers will start kicking down just to impress her, and I'll actually make some cash tonight.

But then she pulls her sunglasses off and pushes them up into that long hair, and you see the sunlines around her eyes, the ones that belie her well-toned body and her Old Navy outfit. I suddenly realize that not only is she old enough to drink, she's nearly old enough to be my mother. Looking from the back, you'd prob-

146

ably never realize that black miniskirt was years and years too young for her. The guys around the bar realize it too—Larry lets out a noise, something that's a cross between a grunt of excitement and a sigh of resignation.

I start hoping she'll sit in my section, and then hoping she won't. I'm tongue-tied around women in general, especially older women. And while women my age think that my shyness is cute and sweet, and all one big put-on, I know this woman's going to see right through it.

Plus, this is a family place. Kids lolling around, throwing fries at the next table over while their father escapes into the bar for a quick one, and the mother sits at the table scarfing the burgers that the kids don't eat. We never get any real action here, other than the occasional wife who's had a few too many and realizes she's been waiting around for twenty years for her husband to notice her, and who suddenly needs everyone in the bar to tell her that she's still really pretty.

The other reality is this: older, beautiful women are the ultimate bitches, especially when it comes to those of us who serve them. I've been waiting tables, mixing drinks, and scanning groceries long enough to be wary of anyone who walks in looking like that. She looks around, and I think, *oh, duh, she's waiting for someone.* But this woman doesn't look like the mommy type. And she's definitely not the poor-me type. Then she sees me, flips her long brown hair over her shoulder, and clicks my way in her pedal pushers.

"Where's your section?" she asks, loud enough to make the guys at the bar raise their eyebrows.

"O-over there," I say, pointing to the corner table. Of course, my section is bigger than that—there's no one here but me, so I've got the whole damn place to myself

—but if she is going to treat me like her cabana boy, I suddenly don't want the whole damn world to know about it.

"Well, come get my order then," she says. Now, I hear statements like that all day long—tough men who think they've got something to prove, women who think that anyone who works in the service industry pretty much amounts to their hired help. But the way the words purr out of her mouth, it's like an invitation I can't refuse. I'm the rat, and she's playing me like the pied piper.

"What can I get for you?" I ask, trying to look into her eyes and not into her shirt. She pulls a cigarette out of her pack, and I pull the Bic out of my pocket (it's a "uniform" requirement here, just like pants) and light it for her.

"Service." She says. It isn't a question. "I'll have a Sex on the Beach."

"Oh," I say. I rub my palms down my pants. I have a bad feeling about this already. "We can't actually serve that here."

She squints at me through a haze of cigarette smoke, and raises one perfect eyebrow. "You can't serve me Sex on the Beach?" she asks, and although it sounds like an innocent question, the absence of the word "a" is enough to make me dizzy.

Suddenly, more than anything, I want to say yes. But I can't. Instead I just nod.

She leans closer to me. "Is that a yes, you can serve me? Or a no, you're declining to serve me?"

"No," I say, not answering her question at all.

"But this is a bar, right? And you've got juice and alcohol, right?" I'm nodding like one of those dogs you see in the backs of cars with their heads on a spring. "Then mix them together and make me a Sex on the Beach. Please."

Oh God. "Um, I can make you a Fun on the Beach." My voice is barely a whisper, and I'm starting to wonder why I don't just throw Mr. Manager's stupid rules out the window and make her the damn drink.

"A. Fun. On. The. Beach." She says the words so slowly she seems to be tasting them.

"We're a family place," I say. I've had this drilled into me since day one. I know this line so well that it starts coming out, even when I don't want it to.

"I see," she says. She smiles, and I smile back, suddenly relieved. She's going to order something simple like a gin and tonic, and I'm going to make it for her, and everything's going to be fine. But, then she leans toward me, and there's this glint in her eye . . .

"So, can I get a Slippery Nipple?" she asks. I can feel my cheeks growing warm. I shake my head. "Probably not even a Satin Sheet," she says. Her voice is getting louder. Out of the corner of my eye, I see the guys at the bar crane their heads around. "How about a Muff Diver?" she asks. Her fingers are toying with her lips, and there's the faintest smile playing across her features.

She leans in closer, until her lips are nearly nudging my ear. "Or maybe you could give me a . . ." she lingers, her breath resting against my skin. ". . . Screaming Orgasm?" My legs have begun to tremble, and the whole time she hasn't even touched me. I don't dare look down, but I'm suddenly glad that an apron is part of my uniform.

"No," I say. My voice is ragged. "Not that either."

"Well, I seem to remember something else on your menu," she draws back a little, seems to be mentally searching for something. I suddenly feel her calf against mine, and pray to God that the guys at the bar are staring at something on the TV. "A little concoction with Amaretto and raspberry liqueur. What was that drink, do you think?"

I'm zipping through the list of drinks in my mind, trying to remember all the ones with those ingredients.

"Wet Dream?" I say, stupidly. It's the first one that comes to mind. "Almost Heaven? Lobotomy?" I'm starting to think I might need one after all this is over.

Finally, she sighs and leans back against the chair. It's apparent that she's given up on both of us. "Oh, forget it," she says. "Just make me a strong cocktail."

It's only when I get back behind the bar that I realize what she had asked for. *Duh.* I can tell it's too late now, though, so I'll just mix her something simple, and forget about it. But then one of the guys at the bar leans forward, and gives me a wink that says go for it.

And suddenly, I realize that I want to. I pull the Amaretto and the raspberry liqueur from the shelf, mix the other ingredients in, and head over to her table. I slide in the chair across from her as I set her drink down.

"I think this is just what you asked for," I say.

She looks up, surprised, and then breaks into a wide smile.

"Yes," she says. "It is." She takes a sip of her Fuck Me Hard, and I head to the back to let my manager know that I'm no longer going to be serving.

At least, not here.

Divining Rod

Robert Gibbons

I'll grasp the wooden handles of the divining rod & trace
the subterranean days of forty years of your life.
First memory: Marilyn Monroe's death
the same year your father died
when you were too young
to attend the funeral.
Her public mourning
replaced your
private loss.
Questioning his absence must have been a constant,
stinging refrain sung by you & your twin,
never supplanted in meaning
by the brilliance
of the language
yet to come.
Remember you read the epilogue to *Moby Dick*
on the Custom House stairs
in Salem before an enthusiastic crowd?
They stayed around to witness your spontaneous
sibilants, well-rehearsed plosives,
sun accentuating yellow hair,
dark glasses shielding
a deep sensual
mystery
in one page,

as if the actress had been cast in a lone serious role.
Talk about *Misfits*, they say Gable went down
before the goddess,
DiMaggio,
Miller,
your whole family, too,
marks a long line of male graves.
Two guys had to pull you out of your first husband's
mother's house in Chula Vista, California,
guns drawn, otherwise,
he never would have
let you go.
Who could blame him? That skin, those
eyes, the intelligence written across the face.
On your thirty-first birthday I told you we were through,
you were all too much. Whereupon you heated raw
your naked sex under the sun & drew me
to a cave where you wailed a long, grieving
orgasm which became the glue
between us.
They can't pry us apart now!
Julia Kristeva's *Tales of Love* saved us,
especially her theory that love's crisis
turns words into a work-in-progress.
Invited guests of Piper, because we sometimes wrote
about wine, & loved champagne, every guy
in Cannes wanted to dance with you.
You obliged, but rarely
took your eyes off me.
There's something about the mimosa out our seaside window
meshing with the image of you in black bra
putting on black stockings clasped
to black garter belt when
they knocked

on the guestroom door to hurry us up
for the premiere
of *Les Patriotes* with Sandrine Kiberlain
at the Palais des Festivals.
The paparazzi caught you on those red-carpeted stairs,
hair still wet.
Back in Washington they all would have gone to war
if they thought for a minute
you'd submit.
Even now, five days from your fortieth birthday young
& old wax sonorous in your presence.
But you keep me on.
I can only guess why.
The other day I said I'd rather give you an orgasm than a
house.
You quoted it back to me the next day on the highway
just when a car passed us doing eighty with bold
lettering & a local phone: GOLDEN HOUSE.
The *Golden Lotus* is considered by many
the greatest Chinese novel,
though its blatant pornography stands in the way
of full critical acceptance.
Here's my gift at the birth of your maturity: thumb on belly-
button, one or two fingers around your anus,
my eyes lighting up the fork below
your torso, tongue in
praise of your
wonderful
cunt.

Grizzly

M. Christian

"Taking a walk in the forest," he used to say, thin fingers strolling through Rocky's thick chest hairs. It was a little joke, stretched way beyond humor into an endearance between the two of them. Later, into their first year together, Paul used to add, "—and there's the mountain," when he got to Rocky's dark red, crinkled nipples, and "—the cave—" when he got to the big man's navel.

Paul had tried to think of something else to continue to the tour with—maybe "the pale tower," or "the great peak," or even "the mighty column"—but just shortly after that they'd had their first fight, and then they weren't together again.

Months after, Paul found himself missing that forest, those mountains, that cave, and—more than anything—walking there with his bear.

Rocky used to come with his own forest—but not just the pelt on his broad chest. Paul could see that, even before he knew the big man's name: primordial wildness seemed to follow him like his shadow, the howl of wolves lingering after he'd finished speaking.

Considering that Rocky was a graphic artist for a stylish queer magazine, that was quite an accomplishment. But looking at him—that first time at the Shindig Dance after the Folsom Street Fair and every time after —Paul could see it, despite the contrast between person and occupation. Rocky carried the forest, the wild, with him—a kind of untamed aura, a ferocity of life that made more civilized men feel the tiny little hairs on the back of their necks stand on end. For Rocky clothes seemed to be an unnatural state, even through he wore them well. You could look at him in his fine leather cowboy stompers, his so-tight jeans, his denim shirts (sometime with Navajo flattened dimes for buttons) and know that this was not a natural state for the man. No, he needed to be standing tall and proud under the buttresses of some mighty forest, a carpet of pine needles under his mischievously furry feet. Nature was Rocky's demeanor, his flavor, his scent. He was a great bear, a magnificent bear, that while he had trained himself to walk on two legs, dance, hold a day job, go to Costco, hold a long-necked beer, and all the other trivial refinements of "culture," it was obvious that this was just skillful training. Beneath this costuming he was a great, furry beast.

—and he turned Paul on, something fierce.

There was that wildness—that scent and demeanor —but there was also ferocity. After that Shindig Dance— Paul moving hesitantly to the music, Rocky more dynamically, as if the country beat were pulling his strings —in Paul's tiny SOMA loft, Rocky's kisses had seemed more teeth than lips, as if he growled his excitement, rather than purred like so many of Paul's tricks had done. Clothing hadn't *melted off* as in high romance (or light porn) but rather tore free, pulled aside by Rocky's stern, determined foreplay. Paul remembered the ricochet of buttons and the tearing of damned-untearable jeans.

Through the coppery taste of fear, Paul had been turned on—Mary, Jesus and Joseph he'd been turned on:

his cock had seemed more like metal than meat. His dick, that too-hot September afternoon (as all Fair days were) had strained, pulsed, throbbed, ached (as in low porn, for the first time the cliché having meaning) as Rocky had roughly jerked him off, great bear-mitt enveloping even the trembling length of Paul's quite-proud cock.

Then Rocky's jeans had been parted, his threadbare cut-offs pulled down and off—revealing a great, purple-headed cock, already beaded with pearlescent excitement. "Suck me"—not a bark, but rather a rumbled tundra demand. Bear in appearance, bear in nature.

Paul had almost choked, that first afternoon—he'd nearly impaled his head on the so-firm member in his eagerness to taste, feel, surround Rocky's big cock. He remembered, dimly, the blast of pleasure that had red-dened his cheeks (both sets) as the great bear had rumbled his excitement over Paul's cocksucking technique. More red, more warmth after a few minutes when Rocky's big mitt had descended onto Paul's shoulder, and the words "—I'm gonna fuck your ass—" had thundered down from above.

Paul's ass was candy, someone had once said, a frilly old boyfriend who had betrayed his lisping appearance by being—for Paul—way too rough in bed. At first, Paul had taken the word to be a kind of compliment, some-thing nice wrapped in a sarcastic aside. It wasn't until later, prissy banter at a party, that Paul realized the tender-ness he needed, wanted, was being slammed. His ass was candy all right, sweet—but also immature and dainty. Not hot, not wild—dainty.

But that day the copious amounts of lube he usually asked for, usually demanded, the slow, slow, slow build up, maybe even the start with the little buttplug was all .. . forgotten. That day, the thought of pain, the fear of tear-ing, of letting go—well, it all kind of let go. So when that avalanche of deep tones tumbled down from Rocky ("—I'm gonna fuck your ass—"), all Paul thought was how fast he could turn around, and take that big cock between his cheeks.

The sensation had been beyond pleasure—beyond pain, too. It had been some incredible combination of both. Never had Paul been so excited . . . and, afterward, when he felt the diving heaviness of Rocky's balls unload their hot come in his ass, Paul had never felt so ecstatic.

It wasn't until later that the fear had started. A little at first—then, later, much more.

Their relationship began with that hot afternoon, and lasted almost until the next, two months later. For Paul, it was a magical time—many walks in the forest (Rocky's chest hairs again), up to the mountains (nipples), and the cave (navel). And many special journeys to the big man's cock, that had always defied geographic metaphor. His was just big—damned big.

Many slow weekends and some weeknights, Paul lounged in the big man's arms, stroking his big cock, sucking it, and taking it between his hungry cheeks. Each night, each day, seemed to grow, to build with intensity. Once, and then twice, then more—their times tipped towards fear for Paul. At first it was a biting spice, a thrill of rough, rough, tough blasting comes (from both of them), but then it became an expected part of their time together.

The first time the pain had pushed him beyond his excitement, he'd said, "Please"—to which Rocky had growled, deep and low, slapped him hard and pulled out.

The next time, he'd whispered, "Please, Sir," and Rocky had pinched his right cheek, hard, pulled out and sighed . . . long and low.

The time after that, he'd yelped—a hard, barking sound. Rocky had stopped . . . quiet, gotten up, went to the bathroom, got dressed, and left without a word.

Paul didn't see him again—not until a lucky, fateful day at the Lone Star.

Paul had been wandering SOMA, quietly cruising down the cold industrial streets looking for . . . he didn't know what. It had only been a week or so since Rocky had packed up and silently left his little apartment. At first Paul had hid behind the simple illusion that Rocky had pushed too much, too hard, that Paul had protected himself by stating his limits. But there were other times, times that seem to be submerged in a deep lake of calmness. It wasn't tranquility, rather a kind of stupefying comfort —as if the world had been covered by childhood blankets. He'd tried to jack off, but the smiling men in his videos had seemed plastic, insincere . . . cool, as if their skillfully applied sweat and come was really ice and frosty icicles. His dick remained limp and, like everything else around him, uninspired and passionless.

Chance brought him to the door of the bar, and music drew him in, the crowd—smelling of real hot sweat, real burning sex, kept him there.

He was starting to drift, lose himself to the atmosphere, when recognition jolted him, a 220 current of embarrassment: that forest, those mountains, the cave lost behind the buttoned lower part of his old workshirt: Rocky was sighting down the barrel of a pool cue, eyeing the prospective dynamics of a seven ball when Paul saw him—and then, a heartbeat later—when Rocky saw him.

Flush, cheeks too warm, Paul had turned to go—went —but didn't get any farther than the corner. Rocky's hand was heavy, firm, stern. "Wait," he said in his tundra voice, "hold it right there."

"What?" Paul said, his voice giving up an embarrassing squeak. "What do you want?"

He didn't smile, his face was hard and unmoving, but something trickled through his words like a clever grin. "I'm not the one goin' looking for something this late. You want to go back to your place?"

"Not really, no."

"You liked it before—till you chickened out."

"You were too rough," the words took a lot to get out, but he managed it, nonetheless.

"Bullshit. You just like to say 'no'—it wasn't about being hard, or shit like that. I can tell. It ain't magic or shit like that, but I can tell. There's a difference between real hurtin', being scared . . . of bein' scared." He stopped, looking at Paul with eyes like deep mountain pools. "I guess you just ain't ready to look at yourself and like what you see."

He turned to go, saying "Call me when you're ready," before walking off into the night.

The world became civilized after that. It became routine, expected, and—best of all—safe. The first thing Paul did was build up a thick protective coat of rationalization, adding one layer after another—that he'd made the right decision, that all he needed was to wait a little . . . sure enough, he thought, believed, his passion would return. Eventually, the boys in his vids would smile sincerely again, and sweat real manly sweat. Life became work, some simple little friends, sleep, and . . . well, sleep. Occasionally, he touched boredom—and just as occasionally he felt that cloak of protection like a suffocating cushion.

Then, one day, he was curled in bed, absently masturbating—hand wrapped around his semi-flaccid dick.

It had been a few months since that thumping bar. Rocky had all but faded to a sense of sneering superiority, his brush with rough (too rough?) fucking, and Paul thought it was all behind him.

His cock wouldn't get hard—then it did, but it didn't feel hard. Instead, he felt hollow, empty, like his dick was a little (very little) inflated balloon and not his favorite organ. Then Rocky came closer than two months ago. Paul remembered precisely: they had left a late showing of The Seven Samurai at a tiny Mission District theater. High on Kurosawa and cheap Mexican beer, they'd laughed down the dark streets.

Then . . . then Rocky's rough mouth, scratchy beard on his cheeks, strong tongue between his lips—and Paul had been hard. Not steel, not iron—just hard. Rocky had broken the kiss with a light—yet firm—slap on Paul's cheek. Struck—in many ways—Paul had taken a step back, shock and excitement running rampant through him. Then, in the dim light of that lonely alley, he'd seen Rocky's cock—steel, iron—out of his pants. "Suck me," the grizzly bear had growled.

Of course he had—naturally, as if he'd become in one quick instant just a mouth, a tongue, and teeth. Paul the maw, Paul the born cocksucker.

It had been good. It had been so good (and Paul's cock, back in the present, was hard—very hard), so damned good. He'd sucked and sucked, dying for the taste of his grizzly's come. He'd sucked and stroked his own so-hard dick through his too-tight pants, praying to the great faggot god for Rocky's to spurt in his face.

Then Rocky had pulled him up—his cock popping free like a cock from a bottle. Hard hands on Paul's shoulders, a quick twist, and Paul has facing away—then cool air on his naked ass as his pants were jerked down.

Rocky fucked him, bare and rough in that dark alley

—fucked him harder than he ever had, ever would. Paul's ass was on fire, burning with ecstasy. He wasn't there, wasn't on earth—he was high above the clouds, in some glorious other place.

It wasn't hard, wasn't painful (he remembered, cock very hard in his hand), wasn't too rough, wasn't anything except wonderful. Then, then, then, then—he thought about it. He. Thought. About. It. The fear started, that he'd let go, was wandering without direction. The fear was more frightening than anything that'd been happening.

He'd let the words out, let them slip free. Rocky had stopped, had pulled his cock out (another cartoon pop) and had helped Paul back into his pants. There had been a kind of embarrassed shyness to the big, furry man —but also a kind of frustrated tension.

Now, then, back in his little apartment, Paul realized two things, almost together: one, that was when things had started to go downhill—the fear was too great for him, the terror at what he'd started to enjoy, enjoy too much. That was when it had started to fail between him and his beloved grizzly bear.

He also realized that his cock was hard again—for the first time in months. Hard thinking of that time with Rocky. All it had taken was to remember his grizzly . . . and his powerful growl.

Paul was more than a little anxious that it had been too long, that there'd been too much time between them. But then he'd gotten the call—Rocky was coming.

He knew what was going to happen—and it made Paul smile. He had it all laid out, all ready. He knew it was going to work out, knew it for a fact. Rocky was coming, and for it all to work out all he had to do was walk in Paul's front door.

Paul had taken all the furniture in his place and had pushed it to the side. On the floor, a soft blanket. On the blanket, a basket. In the basket: Little sandwiches, honey, biscuits, some sweets, some good lemonade. Also on the blanket, Paul, naked and smiling.

Rocky was as good as back. He knew that as he knew the sky was blue, the earth round, and that he wanted it rough and hard—as only his grizzly could deliver.

Rocky was back—after all, what bear, grizzly or not, could resist such a fine picnic?

Y Tu Mamá También

Gary Meyer

Between bouts of farewell sex, two teenage lovers preparing to separate for the summer begin a pledge in solemn unison, then break down in giggles:

"I promise not to fuck any . . ."

"Brazilians! Germans! Argentineans! Poles! Venezuelans! Irish! Your father!"

The girl of another parting pair calls down to her boyfriend, marooned in the living room with her disapproving parents, to help her find her passport. As soon as he enters her bedroom, she drops her pants.

So begins the film *Y Tu Mamá También,* Alfonso Cuarón's (*Great Expectations*, 1998) candidly graphic and breathtakingly honest coming-of-age story in reverse. Tenoch (Diego Luna) and Julio (Gael Garcia Bernal), the head-banging buddies anticipating a girl-friendless summer of boredom and whacking off before starting college, have had plenty of sex. Now they need to find out what it means. They're the butt of the joke in which a new mother is informed that her baby has both male and female parts. She asks, "You mean it has a penis *and* a brain?" They rate their marijuana like wine tasters; their manifesto includes: do whatever you feel like, pop beats poetry, and truth is cool but unattainable.

Cuarón made his movie as a Mexican production

because it's inconceivable that Hollywood, which has reduced cinematic sex to a smirking peepshow serving body parts on a platter, would ever have green-lighted it. Consider the scene of the boys reclining on diving boards in a deserted country club, fantasizing about every woman they find attractive. ("How about your girlfriend's mom?" "Fuck off!") The camera pulls back to reveal them furiously masturbating. They come simultaneously; an underwater shot capturing their spunk plopping into the pool.

The woman whose image sends them over the edge is Luisa (Maribel Verdú), the wife of Tenoch's cousin, whom they met at a posh wedding and promptly invited to accompany them on an improvised journey to an imaginary beach called "Heaven's Mouth." After her husband admits to infidelity in a drunken phone call, she calls Tenoch; much to his surprise, the trip is suddenly on. Frantic preparations and map reading ensue: "That's not a road, asshole; it's a river!"

The rapidly shifting power dynamics among the trio prevent easy answers to the question, "Who's having whom?" Not older enough to make this story an intergenerational tale like *The Graduate's* Mrs. Robinson and Ben, Luisa is nonetheless a mentor to the clueless boys, one vastly more experienced in the arts of love: "You don't slurp like it was a lollipop. You have to be gentle. You must make the clitoris your best friend." Quizzing the boys about their girlfriends, she starts the ball rolling by observing that the reason girls go to Italy is for the men. She's acutely aware of the sexual tension on all three sides of the triangle: "What you really want is to fuck each other!" It's almost a turnabout on the faux-lesbianism so rife in mainstream hetero porn, except that the boys are so sexually tone-deaf, they've even missed the attraction they have to each other.

Portraying entry-level sex in all its clumsy fumbling and premature climaxes, the film doesn't neglect mature monogamy and the monotony it's sometimes heir to, as Luisa drunkenly confesses to the boys in an extended scene of genuine sex talk, even rarer in the movies than genuine sex:

"You know how I knew? He tried things on me that he learned from them."

"Like the finger in the ass?"

"For example."

"No shit!"

"But you have to know how. Delicately, with finesse. You don't just jam it up there."

The opposite of exploitation isn't prudery, but frankness. The boys' beauty and Luisa's attraction to it are appreciated as facts of nature, not leered at. Throughout the film, water provides a metaphor for shedding civilized inhibitions and regaining a natural balance, for purification and forgiveness. In a scene of reconciliation, the boys race naked underwater in a small, leaf-clogged pool. The camera follows them back and forth, showing them full-body, hiding nothing—thirty seconds worship of youth and grace and pure physicality—thirty sensual seconds forbidden to appear in any Hollywood product.

Part stoner comedy, part road movie, part magical realism, *Y Tu Mamá También* finds an ironic subtext in the violent division of Mexican society being enforced just outside the boys' bubble of privilege. Like everything else, they're barely aware of it, beyond complaining about demonstrations causing traffic jams and observing that left wing chicks are hot. Obliviously they count bodyguards at the wedding and cruise by police actions, roadblocks, beggars, and the body of a laborer run down because taking the pedestrian bridge would have forced him to walk an extra mile to work.

As insensitive as Tenoch and Julio are, as necessary as their disillusionment is to their maturation, we've all felt their loss; we've all experienced that moment when we learn that truth, while attainable, is far from cool, and that impossible golden beaches fade as rapidly as promises made in bed.

Ceremonies

Gary Sandman

VALENTINE

33. When I thrust

When I thrust my tongue into Valentine's vagina for the very first time, her hand half-rose to her mouth, and she blinked delicately. After a moment, her hands slid onto her gently rounded belly. She fanned her fingers across her modest navel.

I licked at the right lip and then the left lip. As I sucked hard, the inner lips squeezed into my mouth. It was early spring; the smell of the white roses below Valentine's window filled the room. My tongue flicked against her clit, pushing it around. It twisted, shiny now with her juice. My fingers settled onto her thighs. I slid my tongue deep within.

Valentine rocked her head from side to side, lips pursed, pale blue eyes half-closed. She placed her hands on my shoulders and bent forward. After I thrust my tongue inside again, I rippled it over her musky vagina. I ground at her cunt harshly, my face washing in its wetness. She jerked and closed her thighs against my cheeks. I heard someone come into her parents' house downstairs.

I whipped and yanked my tongue within Valentine. She slumped back and listed sideways on the creamy bedspread. When her hands left my shoulders, she began to flush. She smiled weakly, long blonde hair strewn across the pillow, small buttocks flattened out. On her slight, vulnerable breasts her nipples were hard like needles. She put her teeth jagged against her lower lip.

39. Description Two

Valentine's pink cotton shirt. Her breasts small but well-shaped. Arms gently muscled and elegant. Firm and the flesh rough with goosebumps. Ribs rippling faintly, and a neat line between them, where they divided. The skin tanned, with downy hair. Her navel a vertical slit. Her abdomen rounded, though only slightly.

Valentine's white skirt. Her small, soft buttocks. The zip. Sky-blue panties. Her cunt between narrow, slightly boyish hips. Thin, coltish legs. Her ragged tennis shoes. Long, slender toes.

47. List Four

When Valentine had her period, she gave off a vivid smell.

She blushed at the mere sight of my penis. She got very red. Laughing, she covered her face with both hands. Her rounded eyes peered through her fingers. She placed her fingertips over her mouth.

Valentine kept stealing my Doors T-shirt and wearing it when I wasn't watching.

At Marengo High School, in Senior drawing class, Valentine called to me but I didn't answer. So she started to sob.

As I was masturbating, she loped into the room. She saw me and threw her arm over her eyes, cackling hastily.

She stole into the room late at night and woke me with a gesture of her tongue.

I fingered Valentine's old, faded jeans with pleasure. The seat was shiny, and the crotch was worn thin. The legs were somewhat frayed at the bottom. The jeans smelled of her scent. They recalled her curves.

I wet Valentine's thin lips with my stringy semen.

Spit and come soaked the hair around my cock and balls when she finished.

Dreamily, she remarked how she hated it when her panties bunched up in her crotch.

Tiny bruises tattooed her small breasts.

When I glanced up, Valentine, a pom-pom girl, shifted her eyes to me and then away, smiling. She whirled around and revolved her hips, her small behind and short maroon skirt swinging around. As she dropped to the gym floor, she rocked her ass, still smiling.

Valentine and I sat in my pick-up truck, necking. She was drunk. Suddenly she pushed me away and held up a finger. She leaned out the window and as I watched began throwing up.

She sucked my cock for an hour after I came. Her mouth brought me from softness to hardness over and over again. Valentine made my cock sore, her eyes shy.

ROSS

110. I lay naked with Ross

I lay naked with Ross, in a gray darkness, my heart beating hard. Though we had removed our clothes, I still felt very warm and noticed her animal scent, heavy, forbidding. I gazed at her triangle of hair, squat and black, and then I stared across the room, without thought. Wind hissed through the trees outside her Northern Illinois

University dorm room.

Tentatively I slipped my arm over Ross and grazed my lips against hers. Then she returned my hungry kiss. I placed the palm of my hand over her fat, little breast. We kissed again, thoroughly, patiently.

I lay mute for about ten minutes, aware of the warmth of Ross's body. Trembling, I slid my leg over both of hers, pressing my weight against her belly. I flicked an index finger inside her cunt's pliant walls and yanked it up and down. Ross moved convulsively. We exchanged some words, and then my cock, erect against her perinaeum, jerked briefly, almost unnoticeably, wetting the pink cotton sheets beneath us.

A few minutes later, Ross stroked my cock, like a small, wet bud now.

SARAH

149. Sarah, lanky and red-headed
Sarah, lanky and red-headed, another college student, clapped with delight when she saw my penis was hard at last. Giggling, pert breasts bouncing, she scrambled for a condom but tripped.

205. She handed me a note.
She handed me a note. Abruptly she kissed me on the lips, then hurried out the door. I went over to the window-sill, sat down in the sunlight, and unfolded the blue sheet of paper. It was a vivid description of our lovemaking the night before. She was unusually graphic, unconsciously poetic. She used obscenities several times. I noticed the heavy paper smelled of lavender. A thick spray of flowers and leaves was attached to it. Sometimes she wrote me such things afterward.

212. I rested on my side

I rested on my side, one leg bent at the knee. Gently, I caressed my inner thighs and balls. I grasped the shaft of my penis, and massaged it. As my forefinger and thumb rubbed my scrotum, I inhaled deeply and shook my head. My thoughts were about Sarah.

I stroked my swelling penis, then paused. My fingertips massaged my balls lightly. While I caressed my belly and thighs, I inhaled and exhaled quickly. I caressed my penis, then stopped and waited. Bit by bit my body tightened, then relaxed. I grabbed my hard penis again and pumped it up and down. As my balls began to strain, my hand faltered. Then white spunk spurted over my fist thickly, running down my fingers and catching between them.

221. Enthusiastically Sarah rose up on her knees

Enthusiastically Sarah rose up on her knees, grasped my condomed penis and sank herself down on it. As our hair meshed, her warm buttocks curled over my thighs. A blueberry candle flickered behind us, its scent drifting over. The Allman Brothers played on the stereo. I had dropped out of college; it was the night before I was to leave.

Sarah wiggled her wide hips, my penis squirming deep within her. I closed my eyes briefly. As she laughed, her breath hissing in and out of her mouth, she bounced up and down a bit. For a moment, she swayed, her small breasts shifting. Traffic roared by on the University street outside. Sarah lifted up, then fell down my hard penis. She began shifting back and forth from my hips. She moaned softly.

As Sarah rocked on me, her breasts flopped. She paused, slumped back on her ass, then ran a hand through her short, boyish haircut. I started groaning. The candle wavered behind us. After more of her thrusts, I grabbed her hips and arched up to meet her. Our mingled grunts filled the apartment. Sweat pooled on my chest. As Sarah's breathing deepened, her hips accelerated, and she squealed, saliva flying from her mouth. I slammed her down on me. Sarah's head dropped, and her lips sagged. She locked her thighs and moaned as she came. I inhaled, then emptied myself fully inside her.

THE YELLOW KID

232. List Fifteen

The Yellow Kid checked my cock cautiously, out of the corner of her eye, her face tilted up, at Plastek in Woodstock, the factory at which I was working. Then she lowered her head, dropped her mouth open and stared at my groin. Her eyes flicked up to mine. They darted back between my legs. She turned back to the plastic injection machine she was operating.

When I asked her for a date, I found myself concentrating on her long fingers and the emerald rings upon them.

She had painted blue, cross-hatched, on her belly.

The Yellow Kid's scent and stain varied.

She said she felt she was ugly. She said she had crooked teeth. Her Southern accent drew out the consonants. She showed me the blue track marks on the inside of her right elbow. She said her daddy called her the Yellow Kid after a cartoon character.

The Yellow Kid frowned angrily at me before her wide lips touched my cock. After a few perfunctory sucks, she slumped back on her heels and twisted her head away. The Yellow Kid pushed her thick, blonde hair back. She rubbed her hand over her lips once. When she took my cock back in her mouth, her eyes closed and her nostrils flared.

I think she liked to see me coming up the stairs to her apartment with violets and a hard-on.

Since she lay hidden beneath the sheets, I couldn't tell which end was which.

She bent over to pick up one of my oil portraits, then straightened up, wedging her thumbs under her tight, green panties to pull them down over the half-moons of her ass, her broad hips swinging up one at a time.

My buttocks rose and fell between her spread legs, and in reaction her knees swayed up and down.

I finally convinced the Yellow Kid to stop wearing panties.

She bit me.

The Yellow Kid turned a patchy red at the Plastek lunch table. She looked at me funny, a Braves baseball cap pulled low over her forehead.

She jerked her hips slightly as she poked her fingers inside her genitals. After a moment, she produced two shiny metal balls. She rolled them wet and clicking in her palm, then tossed them across the room to me, one at a time.

The Yellow Kid handed me the telephone, frowning. Ross had called me up unexpectedly; it was good to hear from her.

We were making love dog-style. As an experiment, she wrestled her hips at mine; by accident my cock fell out.

In the middle of the night the Yellow Kid put her foot against my ass and shoved me out of the bed to go turn up the heat. I shuffled across the room, then flew back under the covers, where she wrapped her body around mine.

She slouched, amused, one foot daintily up on a

chair, inserting a cherry-red diaphragm.

The Yellow Kid held the telephone out of my reach as, laughing, she tried to set up a blind date for me.

I handed her some pornographic sketches I'd been working on.

As I got out of my car to go into the store, I spotted the Yellow Kid and said hello to her. I hadn't seen her in some time. My throat was gravelly, however, and my voice broke. She looked at me, startled, and passed by. When I returned to my car, she was standing by hers. She mumbled something and smirked.

264. The Yellow Kid strode toward the living room couch angrily

The Yellow Kid strode toward the living room couch angrily, in her cramped Woodstock apartment, and laid down next to me. It was sunny; a summer breeze tumbled through a nearby window. Phil Collins crooned on the radio. We kissed, then she lifted her loose, white T-shirt up over her head. She pulled her hair back roughly into a ponytail. My arms looped around her tiny waist, and her arms linked around my neck. She spoke to me, slurring her words, her brown eyes slitted.

The Yellow Kid clicked open the catch of her jeans and wrestled them off. Clumsily she tugged a thin tampon out. She shoved her jeans to the floor, grabbed a towel from the nightstand and stuffed it under her hips Quickly she wrapped her arms around my neck and swung my lips to hers again. One of her legs flew over both of mine and weighed them down. She put her hand on my hip, then abruptly grabbed my ass.

We kissed again, our tongues flicking, still lying on our sides. The Yellow Kid flipped over and fit her skinny ass against my belly, like spoons. Her left shoulder blade was adorned with a scarlet cat tattoo. She grasped my cock and jammed it between her legs and into herself. I grabbed one of her springy breasts. As she turned her head, we kissed again. I began rippling in and out. The couch springs squeaked. The Yellow Kid moaned and brushed a strand of her hair out of her face. She whispered to me, asking sharply about some drugs she wanted me to buy for her.

I dispatched my semen inside of her, bit by bit. She rocked her hips fast, then slow, then seized my hand, suddenly inhaling. Her legs lifted, and she rolled away. My cock was streaked with blood. The Yellow Kid rose and pulled her T-shirt and jeans on, eyeing me with loathing. She curled up on the window seat. She said she didn't want to see me again.

MARTHE

296. I loved
I loved the things she did in the ear to me.

301. Her strong, once broken mouth
Her strong, once broken mouth had held many things: tongue, cock, word, wine.

308. Marthe smiled
Marthe smiled when I unbuttoned the thin sweater she wore. As I pulled it off, she bowed her head. I shivered. When I cupped her breast, its thick, brown nipple stirred. Downy hair rose on her skin.

Marthe had met me outside North Line Homes, the Evanston group home at which we were both employed. She was a social worker. We had walked over to my apartment through the heat. Sweat had run down our bodies in streams.

But here it was cooler. Only grey light disturbed the

darkness, wafting across the floor. As Marthe took my shirt, it sent her serene face into shadow. Her bell-shaped breast was warm now under my fingers. When I looked at her, her green eyes seemed mesmerized. She touched her auburn hair vacantly, then lifted her arms to me.

After a while, Marthe stopped nuzzling my jawline. She stood in the window's shaft of dust motes and light, then apart from me in the late afternoon shade. Bending, she slid off her jeans. When I held out my hand to her, she slipped her hand into mine. In bed we took hold of one another.

FANNIE

323. In the darkness Fannie

In the darkness Fannie, a graduate student who worked at the home, reached toward me and pursed her long, elegant fingers against my zipper. She tugged my jeans open, snaked her hand inside, and grasped my penis. She drew it out gently, flopping a bit against her fingers. Fannie bent down, her coarse, corn-rowed hair arcing forward. She kissed the soft, pliant tip. Her broad tongue swirled languidly against its length. She sucked the glans past her thick lips, murmuring.

RED CLOUD

344. She lay sprawled

She lay sprawled across the bed so I brought her a cone of red and yellow irises. Smiling, I scattered them across her rounded breasts, which were the color of just fallen snow.

387. Finger
Finger in cunt, tongue on clit.

397. List Fifteen
Delicately, Red Cloud, a poet, fixed a girdle of blue-bells about her naked hips. Her breath smelled of gin.

My hand lay cupped between the legs of Red Cloud's tight jeans; the movement of the Citroen on Paris's Grand Boulevards ring road made her come.

When she climaxed, her cunt curled, then tightened around my finger, and she guffawed loudly.

A tender, black flower gored by a thick, brown root, above the cheeks of her ass, below my belly.

My penis dipped far down into her vagina and tapped the tip of her womb, and Red Cloud flinched suddenly.

Red Cloud bent over the sink, staring out a small window of my St-Germain house, her big pink breasts hanging out of her robe. She turned to me, sipping a whiskey. She smiled, then tried to hand me the whiskey.

It took me a while to get used to sleeping with some-one every night again. I could only seem to nap lightly.

From beneath the green, silk robe, from between her wide, curved breasts, Red Cloud produced a spray of rose plum flowers and presented it to me, smiling sweetly.

I ran my fingers slowly over her big, round glasses, which she had just removed and which were still warm.

Wrapped only in a creamy towel which coiled at her waist, her curly, black hair streaming past her shoulders, she arranged the stalks of dried sunflowers in a vase. She chatted with me in French. I crouched at an easel, paint-ing her. She sat down at a piano and picked out a Laurie Anderson tune. She had stopped drinking.

Sometimes when Red Cloud passed the windows, she would stir the big, clay wind chimes strung along them, then close her eyes, listening to them.

We found ourselves, later, in a field of wild grass, clasping hands, on a hazy summer morning, by the Verdon River, having spoken not at all.

In Rome, perched on a stool, she pulled a length of thick, chunky beads out of her wet cunt slowly. Sipping gin again, she poked them back in. Linked to the beads were tiny, copper bells that rang faintly when she moved them. They had been given to her by an old boyfriend.

She always kissed me like she was making an offering.

As soon as I slapped her rump, she made an "OH" with her mouth. She spun toward me, knocked me down, threw herself on top of me, and began tickling me, hooting.

She carried my semen around inside her.

In the wildflowers of Vosges, Red Cloud and I lay kissing. Later on we lost ourselves in the woods. At day's end she and I stood by a pond, looking at our reflection. After she took her leave, I found a note by my jacket. In gorgeous characters she had written my name. Once again, she was trying to get sober.

She was naked on the floor. She had a wet, red primrose lying over her navel. Drunk again, vomit dribbled from her mouth.

424. Description Thirteen

My penis was long and thick, a deep pink lined with blue. Thick, black hair curled at the root, spreading across and downward. The skin was soft, the core firm. Underneath it ran a thick, bulging vein. A ring of tender skin erupted suddenly into the glans. The tip was shaped like a condottiere's helmet, peaked and arched. A small slit crowned it.

Beneath my penis nestled my two dense, narrow testicles. They were draped in a loose pouch of skin, which was covered by light hair. Veins criss-crossed them.

Red Cloud sketched me, smiling.

486. I kept thrusting

I kept thrusting, popping past a ring of muscles in Red Cloud's cunt. Her skin, particularly around her collarbone, began to get flushed.

I dropped down and nibbled her neck. Slowly I pumped. The Paris Metro thundered underground nearby. It was past midnight. Red Cloud grabbed my face and stuck her tongue in my mouth as my cock rocked from side to side. She groped for my butt. Her black hair was plastered across her forehead. I rose on locked arms and started thrusting more quickly, the ring of her muscles still massaging my cock. Her chunky right leg was half-tossed over my ass. Grunting, she bucked her belly against mine. We rocked faster. My balls strained and strained. We slowed. I tried to pull out my sheathed cock. But she wouldn't let me, at least not right away. She started snickering.

MY LOVER

488. My lover

My lover's light brown hair shone where the sun hit it. She had pearl skin. Her eyes were large and clear. She was plain spoken.

Tested

Marcy Sheiner

Three years later I am still getting tested.
Six months, say the clinicians.
Eighteen years, a counselor friend told me.

At first I felt like a paranoid het
sitting among legions of gay men
at the health center
but now more women are getting tested.

When I tested negative
a month after you died
I was dismayed.
The next time they took my blood
I was terrified, then relieved.
Now the whole thing has become routine
if not ritualistic.
When the needle pierces my skin
I remember telling you:
I regret nothing. Even if I get AIDS
I will regret nothing.
Perhaps you thought me mad:
I wasn't sure.
By then you were hooked to a respirator
and never spoke again.

Except with your eyes.
They crinkled at the corners
when I reminded you
of the morning we'd clung to one another on Broadway
as cabs rolled by until I missed my flight.

The faint bruise on my arm is oddly reassuring.
Until I get the results
I repeat like a mantra my resolve of no regrets.
So far
this
has not been tested.

Man in the Moon

Adrianna de la Rosa

I.

Once she saw the man in the moon from her lover's house. Standing at the windows looking out over the dark sea, she looked up at the face of the full moon and saw what every Renaissance artist saw; the face in three-quarter view for the first time. This might have been enough for her. Her lover stood behind her, holding her wrists at her back, exerting a gentle pressure. Just enough to tell her that she was his and his alone. She craved ownership like this. For years she had been the dusty, unused wife of someone else, and this was to be her break for freedom.

She wanted him to be very far inside of her, not just in her head, but in her heart and body as well. This was the man she planned to let in. She wanted merger. No one had ever gone this far before toward her center. He seemed to care about this, and his small gestures and caresses were designed to inflame and unlock her each time a little further. She realized that no man had ever really been with her so completely before. His whispers left tracks on her skin, subtle heat.

One night he sat behind her, cradling her. He took her long curly auburn hair between his teeth and drew it out strand by strand. She felt herself growing wetter and fuller, like a plant in a hothouse. He told her that she tasted of cinnamon, and bought her oils with that fragrance to anoint herself. At that time she didn't know what it was to come. Men had pounded into her so much with their hard insistences that she had given up on love. An impotent husband had been a relief after this much sorrow.

But now she wanted to be swallowed whole and submerged in desire with someone else. Another writer. Not for dominance and submission, but for equality. For the feminine, made flesh and lustful. He made her quiver. This had never happened before, and since she had not experienced it, she came. She had to ask him if this was what orgasm was, the first time. He planned to help her in her quest to go up what she called the golden staircase. He would take her by the hand, and they would go step by step. Once she saw the stars and was lost in the cosmos, she clung to him as if he were her only hold left. He just smiled.

He was never afraid of her. He would take her anywhere, and at any time, even through blood. He took her on the floor once amidst the broken glass they kicked aside. Time slowed down. His tongue drew small arcs of flame from her lips. A different door unlocked inside of her. In between, they talked for hours. They had to touch each other. It was something in the blood, something in the bone, two parts of a whole made into something larger. When he came, he screamed as if he were dying. She would push pillows up against his face for him to bite. He would try to fathom just what it was that she did to him. Then she would smile.

The moon came and went, tracing its arc over his house by the sea with no curtains. She would lie in its pure white softness, stretched out fully in front of him, wanting him to drink her in. She had never been this naked. All of her was laid open to him like the fullest flower—a rose or a dahlia in bloom. Her legs akimbo under his flickering hands. He told her to spread them wider, and for some reason this didn't bother her. She did as she was told.

He liked to lie over her in such a way that she was cradled by one of his arms, while his other hand traveled the length of her, slowly and deliberately. He spent hours warming her like this, and never once said he was tired. Just relax, he would say. She let go under this spell that he had over her. She could float on this tranquil sea under the moon and forget everything she thought she knew about herself.

He had two entirely different hands. One was the hand of an artist, gentle, its cuticles forming sensitive V shapes, while the other was simply a ragged claw. It was this animal hand that she loved the most. The intuitive way it crept inside of her, opening her, two places at once. Her own hand touched her clitoris in front of him. No embarrassment. Friends. He helped her toward a place she had never been, out of some perverse kindness he would only name as convoluted in the end. For her it was a kind of bliss that the prophets understood. Only Rumi could describe it. Could enter the edges of it. A poetics made of fire . . .

II.

When was it that she chose to reinvent herself exactly? She must have remembered herself. At least the person she once was who knew how to dance and paint and seduce.

Taking a big chance, she had placed a personal ad. There were many replies, but only one stood out. It was from a man who said he had two calico cats. Then he wrote her a little story about watching a cat come into his garden. Of course this cat was a woman in metaphor.

Once upon a time she understood this language. In the end, the cat lay at his feet while he stroked it leisurely. She knew she could be this cat. But the exciting thing was his mind, really.

He seduced her with a pen. He might as well have fucked her with it. She was excited that he could find his way inside her mind so easily. Before they ever met they wrote each other. For weeks. You might say they made love on paper first. By the time they met in the flesh, age and circumstance no longer mattered. It was the inflammation of the mind and soul that counted.

How did it happen that first night? The night she seduced him? Nothing, yet everything was planned, from the shrimp scampi to the bath. When she fled her marriage, she had found a tiny studio. At first she would just go there and sit. She contemplated the bare white walls and the sea of grey carpet. She walked the beach every day. Then she would go home. It took a month before she actually moved in.

How is it that we pick someone? Or is it all predestined? She was at a loss without her accustomed circumstances, her marriage. In this place she was a free agent. There was a bathtub with a Moorish feel underneath an arch. She spent hours there caressing herself and just dreaming. She painted her toenails different shades of pink, and later blue. There was a kind of freedom in this naked swirling in bubbles looking at one's toes by candlelight.

When he came for dinner she had no plans, and yet to be truthful, perhaps she had. She fixed shrimp and fed him on the floor. She plied him with Glenlivet. He smoked a cigar. Then she wanted a puff, which gave him a kind of license to do something. She put him in a bubble bath that had the scent of Spain under a summer moon. She insisted on reading him a poem—"Sunstone" by Octavio Paz. It was important that he understood the existential qualities of this kind of writing. Later she would find out that he had cried while she read to him.

That night she said, "You can sleep here because it is so late, but you can't touch me." He peeled off her unitard in less than a minute. He went everywhere inside of her. He marveled at her wetness and her taste he named as cinnamon. He took all the wrongs and made them right with his tongue while she lay back and just let him do this, have his way with her. How different this was. He licked his fingers and then told her he wanted to shock her.

After this she only wanted him near water. She would find herself panting at the thought of his touch. How did he know so much about her? How could she possibly be this free with him? She had long pushed past the boundaries of convention. She only wanted his tongue to lick her everywhere.

III.

She liked the way that his hands encircled her breasts through lace. In fact, she could have spent hours watching him stroke them. His fingers knew how to find her nipples in the dark. He had a way with them, like a kind of snake charmer. If he had been blind, he could have found them and made them stiffen. This was simply a manifestation of his desire. He felt they were made from pink alabaster, and he told her this constantly. He liked to suckle them and draw them out like little pink pearls. She loved to watch him do this.

At that time she wore a twin strand of freshwater pearls. He was jealous of where these pearls went down into the crease her cleavage formed. Many times he told her he would like to be this necklace. He would trace the slow descent as she grew wet in anticipation of his next move, his still-frame choreography.

She knew he loved breasts. Large ones. She had gone to Victoria's Secret in anticipation of this affair and bought many different bras and panties. Some were lace-encrusted and some were entirely plain. There was something else she bought. A unitard made of black lace. It almost made her come when she viewed herself in it. She looked just like the picture in the catalogue. She wanted him to see her in this and put his fingers up into her through the veiled slit which was discreetly open between her legs. The place where she secretly foamed for him. She wanted him undone, with his fingers up her ass and her pussy through this little slit, this planned rending of the fabric sheath. Thinking about this made her very wet.

It is always like this in the beginning with a lover, isn't it? His sharp intake of breath when he views her nakedly in those early moments. This corresponds to the equally sharp and jolting sensation just behind and lower than her navel. This is where her pussy holds its breath, waiting.

What is more delicious than thinking you have undone a man?

She did this over the dinner that he made for her. Crab legs and artichokes that first time and she was so wet, she was oh so very foamy that she didn't even care when she opened her jacket and said that she had a little something for him and it was this glistening bra, completely transparent, with leopard print spots, and she waited for his breath and his glittering eyes to return to normal, and she knew she had him right then and there, pinioned.

What she really wanted in that moment was for him

to take her, pushing her back up onto the table with her legs spread so wide that anyone could have seen her pink lips glistening and foaming at the nether mouth for him, and she wished that all his friends could just be outside the curtainless windows watching as he took her slowly and she screamed. She wanted to be this open.

Instead, he never missed a beat as as she stood up and slid her panties off and placed them on the table next to the cracked crab shells. He knew how to make her wait. But it was a kind of dance they did around the edges of the fact that she really wanted him to fuck her right up the ass, her breasts pushed into the remnants of the crab shells and his tongue rimming her and going in and out like crazy, but she would never say this to him. It wouldn't be ladylike, and yet she wanted him so far up there that she could scream and beg for mercy and still he would keep on pushing until he reached someplace that broke inside of her and she was his, all his forever.

But that isn't what happened exactly. She knew she had him by his eyes, and the discreet placement of her panties near the crab shells, and it was all silent. He never said a thing or missed a beat, and yet when he took her that night on his maroon sheets, another place inside her opened.

Sleeping With Commas

Susannah Indigo

I live with a trio of muses who shadow my days and punctuate my nights. They all live *right inside* their sexuality, and insist that I live there also, or at least try to write stories that are right there. All three are entertaining enough that I am rarely found watching television, and I am never bored—give me my desert island choices and I'll take the muses in my head, paper & pen, and a bit of music to keep me from going mad with them. My trio of voices are all dancers, dreamers, poets craving sensual transcendence with not a single concern for the real world. They are the muses of *sudden sunlight and unsettling questions*, and though they occasionally come to me in images, mostly they come in words, in sentences, in passionate phrases, complete with titles and commas and endings.

The muse of my darkest desires is named Velvet. She wears short skirts and a red leather collar, and she is the one most often present. She insists that I look into the shadows of desire and write what is there. She is into dominant men and women, thinking of herself as a lost little girl, obsessed by intensity, emotional truth, and leaps of imagination. She is the muse who helped me learn how to write the secret things that seem so outrageous in your head, but once you get them down, it's just another story and not so bad after all. She asks questions over and over again during the writing—*what is this about? is it true? does it matter?* When she is present I listen to music like the soundtrack to "Twin Peaks" on headphones to keep her there—she often cries, never laughs, and thinks of herself as *going mad from roses* —but still, she makes me write. I discovered Velvet living quietly in my subconscious, just waiting for my attention, due to a man I was wildly in love with, a man I wanted to be able to express intense thoughts to. They worked in combination for a while, but she has long since pushed him aside, taken control, and she is a more powerful force than anything else in my life.

Fortunately she has a sister muse who thrives on humor. My muse of *sex & laughter* is named Isabella, and she comes to me in the middle of my ordinary days and whispers things like, "Did you know that zucchini make the best cocks?" Isabella is the muse of *perfect cherries*, of *upside-down sex*, of *chocolate dreams*, and she is always dancing away from hot lovers, often leaving them pining in her wake while she's looking for what's next. I listen to the Grateful Dead on headphones when she is present, and together we dance out the silliness into stories that are meant to delight, yet still tell some truth about the passion and absurdity of our erotic lives.

A sad man completes my trio, and he is the muse of *longing,* the muse of *men left behind by beautiful women*, the muse of *sad Frank Sinatra songs in the middle of the night*, the man who will never quite recover from his romantic losses. His name is Miles, but he has Al Pacino eyes and a Richard Ford/Tom McGuane kind of writing voice. It is always 92 in the shade for him, and he's confused and *tangled up in blue* about why things are the way they are. This male voice is not a voice I would ever practically choose to write in, but it is a wonderful way to get at the stories of certain women who cannot tell their own tales because they are half-crazy and could never tell the reader anything that was true.

Invention is my vice, and my muses know this. We are not good friends—they often invade my time in troubling ways. I am grateful that they are only present one at a time. I am friends with them only in a bit of a *folie à deux*, supporting each other's madness and delusion, reaching for the zone where the words and the ideas and the images all blend together into an authentic tale, and then I am grateful when they go away and I can return to being a normal grown-up in my ordinary life—a mother, a businessperson, a practical soul, a woman who always seeks out the sensual in books & movies yet isn't obsessed by them. But if my muses stay away too long —if my dreams become a blur and there is no grammatical decadence or wild passion coming to me—I begin to miss them, and all I have to do is put their music on my headphones and maintain my disciplined two hours a day of writing time, and I know they'll come dancing back with tales of heat and laughter and love.

The Lovers

Dorianne Laux

She is about to come. This time
they are sitting up, joined below the belly,
feet cupped like sleek hands praying
at the base of each other's spines.
And when something lifts within her
toward a light she's sure, once again,
she can't bear, she opens her eyes
and sees his face is turned away,
one arm behind him, hand splayed
palm down on the mattress, to brace himself
so he can lever his hips, touch
with the bright tip the innermost spot.
And she finds she can't bear it—
not his beautiful neck, stretched and corded,
not his hair fallen to one side like beach grass,
not the curved wing of his ear, washed thin
with daylight, deep pink of the inner body.
What she can't bear is that she can't see his face,
not that she thinks this exactly—she is rocking
and breathing—it's more her body's thought,
opening, as it is, into its own sheer truth.

So that when her hand lifts of its own volition
and slaps him, twice on the chest,
on that pad of muscled flesh just above the nipple,
slaps him twice, fast, like a nursing child
trying to get a mother's attention,
she's startled by the sound,
though when he turns his face to hers—
which is what her body wants, his eyes
pulled open, as if she had bitten—
she does reach out and bite him, on the shoulder,
not hard, but with the power infants have
over those who have borne them, tied as they are
to the body, and so tied to the pleasure,
the exquisite pain of this world.
And when she lifts her face he sees
where she's gone, knows she can't speak,
is traveling toward something essential,
toward the core of her need, so he simply
watches, steadily, with an animal calm
as she arches and screams, watches the face that,
if she could see it, she would never let him see.

Photographic Memory

Mike Kimera

The camera never lies. It is we who . . . elaborate.

One sentence and he has their attention. By the end of the lecture he will have their devotion—as he has mine. Poor Philip. So many devotees and so little idea of what to do with us.

He makes a fine figure at the front of the lecture hall, dressed in black, only the shocking white of his hair and the bright blue of his eyes daring to add color to his sobriety.

When he faces his audience, each of us feels that we alone are at the center of his gaze. We are pleased to be there.

His voice is rich and sensual. The serpent spoke to Eve with such a voice.

Behind Philip, uncommented on and therefore powerful, a series of photographs flash on the screen. One shows a woman in tears beating her fists against a man's chest. What a brute that man must be. Then the same image is shown set in a broader scene that reveals the funeral which has prompted the woman's grief. The next shows two lovers in a passionate embrace, but the zoom reveals them as actors on a stage. Image after image draws us in and then casts us off.

In the coming weeks, you will learn how to see, so that you can lead the elaborations of others.

He is inviting them to be special, like him. Offering them the ever-vacant post of sorcerer's apprentice. Some are leaning forward to drink him in. Others are eagerly writing down his apparently spontaneous words. Most of the class are women. All, except me, are under thirty. The few men in the room must already feel excluded or outshone.

The images stop. The screen goes blank. We look expectantly at Philip, who stands center stage in all our minds.

The art of photography is to use a lie to tell a truth.

He smiles. The smile says, I know. A disturbing idea too glibly put. But forgive me. We both know that humor and truth can be co-habitants for a mind quick enough to tell them apart. Smile. Show me you understand.

Almost everyone is smiling now. We are sharing the intimate wisdom of Philip Clarke, an artist who recognizes us as being cut from the same cloth as himself.

I glance around the auditorium, trying to guess which women Philip will allow to worship him this term. Perhaps the one with the pre-Raphaelite hair will be his Beatrice? Or the tiny Japanese girl? Or the tall slim one whose handsome face and upright bearing speak so clearly of strength? Or the wholesome blonde, who looks so much as I did when he first took me to his bed?

Philip continues to reel them in with his words and pictures, but I have slipped his hook for the moment. I stop listening and just watch him. We have been together for fifteen years now, Philip and I. In all that time what has he taught me to see, other than himself? What elaborations has he led except to weave me into his life so that I no longer exist separately from him? How often has he lied to me to be truthful to our marriage?

Unbidden, a pop song that Philip would wrinkle his

nose at slides into my mind and refuses to leave: "If you wanna know if he loves you so, it's in his kiss."

That was how he caught me the first time, with his kiss.

I was twenty-two, beautiful, invincible, and about to be swallowed whole. His hair was black then, and his clothes were colorful. When he stopped me on campus, wearing his ever-present camera like a talisman, and asked me to pose for him, I laughed. An older man (thirty seemed so old then) asking to take my photograph? Next he'd be inviting me home to look at his etchings.

I struck a lascivious pose and said, "Will you make me your Playmate of the Month?"

"No," he said, without a hint of humor, "I will make your beauty immortal."

From another man the words would have sounded pretentious; Philip made them sound truthful.

I dropped my silly pose and said, "Okay, how do you want me?"

At last he smiled. It felt wonderful to see him smile.

"Follow me," he said, and I did.

Being photographed was hard work. Philip wanted only my face and he wanted it just so; with the light like this and the expression like that. He took photograph after photograph. The only sound was the camera shutter applauding his efforts.

The final pictures were taken from very close up. The lens seemed to be sniffing at me like a dog. When he lowered the camera and looked at me, I thought another adjustment of the lighting would follow and I stayed immobile. Then I realized that he was filming me with his eyes, engraving me on his memory. It was impossible to look away from him. He brought his face closer and closer and then he kissed me.

I had been kissed before, many times: flirtatious

196

kisses, passionate kisses, eager kisses; but no one had ever kissed me like this. This kiss was a contract, a promise. It was a connection that couldn't be broken; an indelible brand that changed who I was.

The sex that followed was an extension of his kiss. Philip stripped me and pinned me to the floor, entering me without asking, holding my arms out cruciform, letting me writhe and struggle but making his cock the pivot of my world.

My previous lovers had made gentle, attentive love to me. Philip fucked me.

When it was over I was crying. Crying because it was over. Crying because I knew he would leave me. Crying because no one would ever fuck me like that again.

Philip kissed away my tears and said, "Come with me to India."

I walked away from Cambridge and my PhD to follow Philip. I was obsessed with him. I could see nothing but him. For ten years I traveled with him around the world, seeing what he saw, being his model, trying to be his muse. I was addicted to him, not just to the visceral thrill of the sex, but to his hunger for life and for me, his exhilaration at his own powers, and most of all, his optimism. We were lotus-eaters, drinking in the world like nectar.

Our dreamtime came to an end two years ago in October. When Philip left me in the pre-dawn dark of that autumn day, I was dewed with sweat, sated from his attentions, and all was well. The next time I saw him everything was broken.

Philip was on the Great Western train that crashed at Ladbrook Grove, killing 132 people. They found him wandering amongst the dead and dying, taking photograph after photograph. He was unhurt except for cuts and bruises. When they returned him to me later that day, I kissed him and held him, declaring him to be my Lazarus. He tolerated my embrace and then excused himself to go and develop his film.

I lost him over the next few weeks. He would shout in his sleep and then deny having had the nightmares I wanted to free him from. At first he wouldn't touch me, then, when we did fuck, the sex was laced with anger or blighted with semi-impotence. He started to sleep alone. For the first time since we'd met, my bed was empty.

Philip never talked about the crash. He locked the photographs of carnage away and stopped carrying his camera.

When he decided to take the post of artist in residence at the university, I hoped it meant he was recovering. In a way he was: he gave wonderful lectures and displayed his works with pride. He also started fucking his students. He knew I knew, but we never talked about it.

I wanted to ask him what he was getting from those young women that he didn't get from me. I don't think it was just that they were young and eager. Maybe it was the way they saw him. The same way that this new crop of students are seeing him today.

Truth needs distance, not context, Philip says. *People in photographs taken five years ago can look more alien than people whose images were captured a hundred years ago. Context distracts, distance provides focus.*

I try to extract Philip from his context—husband, lover, friend—and see him, just him. He is an older man, still charismatic, maybe a little vain, a little too carefully presented. I watch him pace and gesture and I realize that there is no real interaction between him and his audience, no creative push. This is a rote performance, rehearsed spontaneity. This is no longer a man who drinks in the world, but one who shuts it out. His eyes look not outwards but inwards. And they look sad.

I wonder if perhaps Philip fucks his students not because they worship him, but because they don't really see him at all.

The camera is a machine for trapping time. Flypaper for moments of truth.

This part of Philip's lecture is new. And there is something in his voice now. An echo of the man who said, "Follow me," and kept me constantly in his wake.

Each photograph, Philip says, *is a time capsule. A message in a bottle.*

He is looking directly at me now, and doing it so obviously that heads are turning toward me to see the object of his attention.

The message you send is up to you. It could be sex?

A picture of me, the first picture he ever took, appears behind him. Some students make the connection and look back at me.

It could be death . . .

A rapid sequence of pictures from the crash, all shown with merciful brevity.

Or it could be hope.

The last picture is of me. It has been taken very recently. I am asleep, alone in our big bed, hugging a pillow. I look every year of my age.

Everyone is looking at us now, their eyes going from Philip to me and back again. Philip is looking straight at me, apparently oblivious to the rest of the audience that he is addressing.

But remember one thing, it is not the message you send that counts, it is the message that is received. Photographs are like memories, they mean nothing unless they are shared.

The room bursts into applause. I try hard not to cry and don't quite succeed. Philip stands still, waiting.

I walk down the steps of the auditorium to meet him. When I am close enough for only him to hear I hold out my hand and say, "Follow me."

And he does.

Baby Eats Hearts

William Dean

Baby eats hearts in the City of Lost Angels. She wears leathers every Thursday, and today she wears red suede hearts that pulse when she walks. When she wears leathers, her voice dips low and husks over with the glossy scales of reptile lust. Her eyes are neon-snake eyes; her lips are ruby blood red; Baby is looking for *luv.*

The City of Lost Angels is webbed over with black lace—ruin, acid-eaten, shattered window and splintered souls. The spiders of sex tune the strands; ride the wind; chant the magic in the deep nights of L.A.. Baby smiles as she drives there; top down; wind-blown hair; no panties. *Come on, Nite. Baby wants loving.*

Hearts pulsing on February 14 rain the beat of lovers' desires like gasoline teardrops waiting to ignite. *Voodoo luv is here.* Ancient Cupid once more, for eternity, seduces Psyche; naked feather on goddess skin; the golden blinding caress of Apollo; the rabid kiss of satyr; the surrender of Dryad and priestess; *luv.*

Baby knows Cupid lives down in the jungle; where the Crazies reign and the homeless prey; down in the tunnels and the ruins; down where the Gods party in chaos and madness and murder and money. Baby wants *luv* real bad. *Luv, luv me,* Baby says over and over. Baby wants *Erotik. Exotik.* Baby wants to cream her leather jeans and for Cupid to hit her with his best shot. *Luv rulez.*

Baby wants her body painted with the graffiti of living desire; fiery kisses and burning hungers; scrawled on by the random tongue, pulsing in the music of the raw, animal fucking. Baby wants writhing; she wants *Art.* Her mind walls are splashed with Gauguin seductions and Van Gogh eruptions of skin and semen and sweat that blot out the fine lines of lover and loved. Cupid watches her walk through the rubble and his eyes are like Father Sun; as hot and light and blinding as *luv.* Baby touches him.

It. Burnt. Out. The City of Lost Angels falls into Darkness. Shadowed lusts rise like smoking wisps from dying fires, where huddled tormented haunted things wake into the Night. Cupid in eclipse; Baby unveiled. Fallen angel wings caress her in a Damnation Game of immortality in *luv.* Baby is hungry for heart, for lips, for his perfect mouth, his smooth strong body. Baby wants a valentine. *Now.*

Baby wants his *erotik* mind to harden and take her; into the sky; off on a vanishing cloud; up to Heaven. Cupid is a god; built like a god; as ravishing and driven as a god. Baby wants her mind to empty and fill with him. Baby can't afford it. Baby wants but isn't ready. Baby is afraid suddenly. *The power of luv.*

Cupid's voice is Vox harsh, guttered with static and thunder; god-writ scripture of desires spill from him as if from a fountain. Baby bathes in his words, splashing his barks and howls and whispers and sighs over her naked arms. Cupid is a whirlpool pulling Baby into promised lace and lavender afternoons in sunlit matings on polished wood floors in June; Baby touches herself, from womb to clitoris, with Cupid's wing. The Lost Angels watch, fascinated as gargoyles, the eyes of the city close, and the city trembles.

In the City of Lost Angels, Baby's scent is musky and sweet. It's a smoggy perfume, dense and smoky, that wakes the Dead and brings out the mad dogs from their caves.

Baby, what luv you unleash, Cupid rumbles at her ear. His tongue—long and wide and pointed—rims her ear skin and darts inside; she feels him tap her eardrum in sudden scarlet whispers of wanting her; wanting her now; wanting her here; wanting Baby's best fuck. It is *Luv Day.*

In Baby's mind, landscapes of pearl lace and red satin hearts swim above the sea of *luv* below; tide and ebb until the World of Baby is all *luv's* pictures, sounds, feelings, and she is happily lost in her own smiles. Cupid grasps her hard, taking her like a king takes a woman or a nation or a single rose from royal gardens. Cupid's muscles envelop her, enfold her, rub her in secret strokes that awaken her every nerve. *Input erotik.*

Like *Ofelia*, awash in dying torrents; like mermaid; like siren, Baby sinks under the wet silk of her sea of *luv*. She drowns in the good liquid suspension, as if arriving at last. *Ecstasy.* Psyche is pulled down into watery couplings; the wrap of weed; the thin moonlit touch almost like froth; the rough bump of denizen; the snarling lust of nightmare. Like *Ofelia*, Baby sinks, smiling.

Slow waterfalls of Cupid kisses adorn Baby's naked pose. She basks, glowing from herself, in *luv's* blindness. Venus and Beauty, her Grace sisters, Fate and Magic, smile and drop their invisible fingers to touch and prompt the coupling. The world is beginning.

Luv rulez.

This is luv? Baby wonders. *It is.*

sundae games

Ceridwen

Shanghai

sunny weekend   lazy pleasures
choose your sundae   this scoop and that
sour and sweet flavours mix and melt
greedy sensations for tongue and mind

pick a man   pick a man
see that soldier stops to stare
as you rub ice cream from your lips
dip in your finger   lingeringly lick it clean
gaze innocently   smile a secret smile
does his dick swell as he longs for your dreamy sucking?

pick a man   pick a man
handsome and mature he
ignores his well-groomed wife
when you slide off your shoe
stretch toes   stroke instep
would he like to bend that arch
feel delicate bones under soft wrinkled skin
bite rosy heel   suck long toes
fill his mouth with your foot   swallow you up?

pick a man   pick a man
suntanned peasant   Sunday best suit
stunned by Shanghai sophistication
let your strap slip   reveal freckled shoulder
stroke your breast   thumb grazing nipple
can he imagine those milky breasts
nipples firm tart strawberries?
could he sink his teeth into this luscious fruit?
do his photos capture your maple-leaf hair
and breasts like juice-filled peaches?

pick a man   pick a man
teenager forgets his friends' girlish giggles
ke-ai   cute   still childish
his mouth round and open he watches
your spoon enter moist lips
does he blush as he imagines you feeding him
then licking ice cream out of his mouth
chilly tongues meeting   eyes speaking wordlessly
of cream-filled cups   sweet sticky juices
melting liquid trickling?

disturbed and aroused   window shoppers move on
intimate strangers implicated in secret delights
you confide to the waiter   I'll have some more
daydreaming indulgence   sundae games

The Suitors

Robert Fawn

It is the the most powerful fantasy of my life as a
transvestite. It is bizarre, as transvestite fantasies often
are. It is difficult to describe, relate, or render under-
standable, particularly since it somewhat confuses even
me. Few transvestites understand the nature of their
obsession. The fantasy is called *The Suitors*.

First, let me ruminate a little about the nature of
the beast. Of ways of viewing reality, a transvestite's is
among the most difficult to describe—because it is all
a fantasy world, a shifting screen of delusive surfaces.
Transvestitism is a long self-absorption. Still, cross-
dressing can answer needs—deep, personal, and, some
say, spiritual needs. The fetish object upon which transvestitism focuses—nonetheless—is the mirror. It is out
of mirrors (the wide bedroom, the oval bathroom, the
coquettish hand mirror) transvestitism spawns. Therein
we first conceive a preference for the image of the opposite sex. A man sees himself, prefers himself instead as a
woman. A woman sees herself, and vice versa.

Transvestites see a gleam in the mirror. That gleam
is a far cry from the ordinary experience of admiring
your own image. We see ourselves other than as we are.
Nor is it true that we despise our natural sex, the sex
we are born with. But the fantasy image is more perfect.

We—this is the best way I know how to describe the fantasy life that swallows us up—experience a life long love affair with an Alice-in-Wonderland dream of passing through the looking glass. This may be a problem. I have never regarded my transvestitism as a neurosis, but sometimes it is simply too much. (I began, like most transvestites, as a child—the cliché of a twelve year old boy playing dress-up in front of his mother's mirror. Yes, it was too intense.)

Caligula-like, that is how intense the pleasures are. They occur within an inverted reality. Transvestites do the opposite of what most people do. Rather than seeking pleasure in pursuit of a male or female sexual partner —a lover—the place where ordinary pleasures lay—we look inside. Gazing down, as though through a funnel, to our mirror reflections. We pursue fulfillment in fantasy identities.

Not in the world, but in the mirror. Fantasy personalities flood through. The flood, once begun, shudders through you as unstoppably as an orgasm. Regardless of sexuality, there are thousands of buried identities in each of us. Transvestitism is a wild, carnivalesque trip that unleashes those hidden personas that wait docilely, under the surfaces, as slippery as water spirits. I will never see them all. Yesterday is never tomorrow. I am never the same woman twice. I dress up as Woman. This is truer than saying I dress up as a woman. While I have distinct fantasies involving special women—oftentimes movie stars, Garbo, Janet Leigh, Debra Winger— I become so many they blur together. Becoming Woman is becoming a legion.

One last point of clarification, before we continue to *The Suitors*. Do not confuse transvestites and exhibitionists. The exhibitionists are the most famous of our kind, but, for each of them, there is a man like me. The man who dresses up in the privacy of a suburban home. The exhibitionists are merely a species. Transvestitism itself in its purest form is a solo performance. For its thrills are those of the mirror, of things one can do with oneself and to oneself. Silk against one's flesh; the opposite sex's underwear; fake, flowing blonde hair. These are self-sensual accessories. It is in the privacy of onanism that transvestitism becomes as obsessive as Hollywood vampirism. Naturally for the public exhibitionists, the drag queens and such, parading about adds a thrill. Many transvestites are simply talented entertainers. Transvestitism, at its root, is still onanism. Exhibitionist transvestites—and I admire them—thrive off the illicitness of masturbating in public.

In the last few years the fantasy that has given me the most pleasure is the moral fable of *The Virgin-slut and The Suitors*. The fantasy dates back from my childhood. I forgot it for many years. But memories from childhood often come back as you grow older. This is one that I am pleased returned.

I usually play the game in the middle of the afternoon. I dim the lights. Sometimes I put on women's clothes. But—does this surprise you?—sometimes not. Transvestitism is a way of thinking, of fantasizing. The feminine accessories, so ostensibly important, only assist a process that occurs in the mind. I enter that deepest, darkest of places, the most palatial of estates: the sexual soul. I can do everything through fantasy, pictures in a shuffled deck of cards. In make-believe, I can wear anything from a nun's habit to a frail pink nightie with a ribbon under the breasts. This was the first women's garment I ever wore. I experienced my first orgasm wearing it. It belonged to my mother. To touch, feel, smell that nightie again is a delicious wish: an impossible, unfulfillable fantasy, just like this fantasy in which men circle around me like horses on a Ferris wheel.

The men are *The Suitors.*

In my fantasies, the women I become wear different faces. But all, all are passive. Easy, pliable. She can never say no. God must be a child-woman like her. This is how God's love shines on earth—indiscriminately. The joy of my perfect woman is how, through her, I can abdicate the world. Every man can drink of me. She offers me a way out. She is free of selectivity, and its ne'er-do-well companion, responsibility. I am freed through her of animosities, envy, guilt, or needs such as to avenge myself, to compete, to get ahead. Thus unburdened, every stranger is a potential friend. I know of no one whom I would wish ungentleness to. I am the world's pillow. This is a fantasy of purity, grace, of drinking long. Come love me . . . relax . . . the world is harsh. . .but ease is as sexual as desire. I heal the turmoil, wrap my legs around the world's anger and meanness. The men who deal with the daily pressure of living thrust up into my belly and find the perfect peace they've sought all their lives.

I part my legs for the anonymous ones. The men —*The Suitors.*

They come. They feast upon my innocence. Strange, dark men. They enter into my palace of illusions. These evil men can try whatever they like—I am an innocent but I will understand, forgive. They can't ruin me. I am holier than they: a complete woman.

The room darkens. Shadows splay, produced by an unknown light source. The suddenness of the change creates a carnival house atmosphere. Cruel men who crawled from Pandora's box don't need to chase me. I lay, like Sleeping Beauty—eyes shut, body tingling. They come. I lounge in a thin dress, naked underneath.

I lower my eyes. They should expect that by now. A woman should always . . . it is like shading a lamp. I have lovers with faces I have never seen.

My first suitor is a well-known movie star. A motorcycle type, he usually appears in movies wearing leather. He strips the gear for me. He kneels in front of me, flexes. He swings his arms up, back, pumps them like fans swinging above my head. He jumps. Agilely kicks off his briefs. I smell cologne when he leans over me. His face is as beautiful as it is on the silver screen, but while he gazes down at me, looking like a child so eager to please me, something happens. Spit dribbles from the side of his mouth. "Boo," he says. Then he attacks.

The next suitor is explicitly cruel from the beginning. He carries a whip, and calls himself Zeus, the God of Thunder. He doesn't want to touch me. He circles me, and cynically snarls, "Look at the boy dressed like a girl, look at the man who thinks he's a woman!" He wants to break the illusion, but I hold on. I feel his nearness like an overcast sky, and as in a dream, suddenly the wind billows and transports me to a weird realm where the shadows of trees sway in a fairy tale forest. This one's presence fills the sky. Lightning flashes; rain falls. His whip cracks.

The third suitor comes to tell me about myself. He is a priest in black robes. He kneels, licks my ear, and talks about love and cruelty. If I would be a woman, I must eroticize the universe. I should abandon the past and renounce my individuality for a world where sex is completely uninhibited. I must embody heaven, hell, and everything in between. He speaks of us creating a perfect world together. That is a world where any man can relax with me, possess me, strip me, violently if he so wants. It should be a joy to forgive cruelty. I should likewise forgive him for what he is about to do. Then he does it.

The last suitor comes to remind me of the woman I truly am, which is no more nor less than an image in a mirror. He is the most unsatisfactory of the four. His hair isn't combed. I suppose you could call him a man, in the generous sense of the word. He looks poor. This one's wrong for me in every important way. His personality isn't particularly flamboyant, nor his face particularly distinctive, nor his eyes satisfactory—usually I like eyes lit with a tiger's fire. He's pudgy. His clothes don't fit, but when I tell him to go away, he smiles. A little too knowingly.

Somehow I recognize him—from the mirror. I tell him this is my fantasy, though he keeps trying to win me with qualities like charm, wit, and intelligence, though in my fantasies only women are witty, intelligent, and so forth. He is really disturbing my fantasy. I want to be the woman. I want to epitomize charm, not be charmed. He doesn't get it.

He sits beside me, talking, joking. He somehow doesn't seem to care that I think he's so average. Then his hands move swiftly to the small of my back and up my legs. I still don't feel swept away—not hard—when this one strokes my panties. He pets my softness through the crotch fabric. I feel nothing. Why do I relax into his arms? Out of politeness. He begins to parlay his feeble attributes to their best advantage though. When he palms my sex flower, what is this feeling, this arousal—it is the rush an old mistress feels when her old man wants affection. He kneels, tickles inside my thighs. Buries his head there without warning me. I clutch his hair. He knew I would like that. He knows everything I like. I am sliding into the furthest regions of fantasy again, all flowers, fawns, and femininity, and when he grabs me and puts his head up my legs I see us as in a ceiling mirror, and he flows over my body and kisses me. I brush my hair from my eyes for him, show him every grace, with exaggerated consent. I am as aware of the positions I assume as a model is when she is being photographed. Even as he unzips himself, I know how my foot arches, how my mouth parts, how he sees me, how the folds of my dress cover my sex flower—until my least attractive lover enters me with a shudder and groans, "Is it good?" And I say his name over and over. "Do you love me?"

He is, of course, me. The me in the mirror. Grabbing his ass, I say, "Yes." "Do you want to see me again?" And I say, "Yes yes," and my legs fold over his hips like a night flower, a long, long . . . *yes*.

The Eastern Philosophy of Sex

Arlene Ang

Scissored by my thighs,
he lectures that Chinese philosophers
created peace between Earth and Water
by warming labial folds with hands.

Don't rouse the sleeping dragon,
I warn him as my fingers close
around wrought iron to fight against
my back undulating on winter quilt.

Snaking over my breasts,
he tongues that firecrackers were used
to scare evil spirits away
and he has just what I need.

Enveloping his theory in pelvic muscles,
I muse that it must have been
New Year's Eve all the time for the wives
and concubines of Chinese philosophers.

Cunt Costumes

Aprill Hewitt

my pussy aims to please
therefore it's always
properly perfumed
primped and
poised in perfection—
it all began when my first man
respectfully requested that i
don a thong for him
and i, wanting to be grown and
dressed for *sexcess* for him
an expensive friendship began
between victoria and my closet
my wardrobe had an affair with sheer
and sky high thigh-highs
there was no more room
for the comfortable cotton i'd always counted on
i never looked back at my
years without cares of underclothes
and i ignored the cries of my
cunt encased in girdles
and contemporary chastity belts
that melted my passion
and imprisoned my pussy
because my cunt costume looked good

eventually though when the
thin thread of $30.00 mock protection
crept through the crack of my cunt
between my ass cheeks
strangling my womanhood
yet again
causing me to come
to the conclusion
that this shit was not worth
the sacrifice of surrendering myself
to a man who worshipped not
my mind
my heart or
my soul
but my feet

well i found a new friend
this time the lovemaking
had me shaking at first
when my man lifted the
suspiciously short plaid skirt
he'd given me and
surprised me with a
quite pleasant smack on the ass
i didn't think twice
when his request came
so i yelled out
Daddy!
instead of his name
now I'll admit this game
was amusing in the beginning
when his fingers pulled my pigtails
i was busy noting the pulling of his
lips on my other lips

between my hips
and his tongue clit-kissing my
clit-tongue
made me begin to sing, but
he placed a musky wet finger
on my moan
silencing me
instantly
and made another request
with foam and a silver sharp razor
he cut God's creation
slicing semen-soaked hairs that
had been coifed so neatly by
another's fine-toothed comb
and my love juice mingled with
blood juice
and he patted my head and said
now you look like
Daddy's little girl
and i thought what the hell
i'll give it a whirl and
exposed my ability to please my man
with my naked vulnerability
enticing him with my
schoolgirl uniform

eventually though the navy fabric
rubbed and chafed and
angry red dots matched round
pink spots on my pissed off pussy
and i was so busy scratching i
lost my passion for the
barber pretending to be my father
and his less than sensuous

shaving caused me to come
to the conclusion that
this shit was not worth the
sacrifice of my lovelocks
so i found a man who didn't care
about my thick hair
as a matter of fact
this Haitian honey's dick got hard
when he spied that even my legs were defiantly furry,
and his
medusa-like snake dreads slithered
beside his tongue
around my nipples
tickling my tummy on his
erotic journey
to discover my body
but his funny bone got harder and harder
to surrender to
now i enjoyed the private moments
we shared
but i cared that each time we went out
my outfit had to be
a severe black suit only
my new, elegant untouchable look
looked great in a book
but I'm a womanly woman and
as i fingered my pearls i considered
1,001 ways other girls were
at that moment having fun
while i was choking underneath
my silk facade

i came to the conclusion
that this shit is too hard
once in a while role-play is fine
sometimes
an aura of mystery is fine
but i want a man who will appreciate
that i don't need to be
spanked smacked or shaved
covered cracked or well-behaved
I'm not a mannequin
but a womanly woman
 so don't ask me on the phone
"what are you wearing?"
but find out who i am, or
go fuck Barbie.

Fuck Dying

Maggie Gray

I fuck the dying.

Certain things are sexy, others erotic. A cellophane-glossed girl, celluloid breasts spilling out of a white lace demi-bra, nipples airbrushed, is sexy. The same girl, wearing a black bra and glasses, sitting at a desk with a book open (below the desk her thighs are open; you can see her fingertips barely touching slickness) is erotic.

Certain things are neither sexy nor erotic. Small fluffy animals. Especially, say, those baby seals on television commercials, begging for your money. Mothers. My mother, definitely.

Old people are taboo, but there's a small niche for elderly porn. This is marketed to other old people and to young people with grandma fetishes. The dead are taboo. Although some must find them arousing, for there is the word: necrophilia.

But what of the dying? Are they off-limits? Those riddled with tumors and God-awful, crying-out pain? I see why they could be a turn-off. But they are still sexual beings. They feel, more intensely. They love.

I fuck the dying.

I work, quietly, through a visiting nurse agency, if you can believe it. The nurses send me e-mails with addresses, diagnoses, the specifics. I don't fuck heart problems. I don't want to kill them.

I'm no hooker with a heart of gold; this is strictly volunteer work and I have another, paying, nonsexual job. And no, I'm not John Irving's Jenny; I'm not trying to steal their seed. Think of me as a cheerleader, or a hospital candy-striper. I bring a too-brief release from the pain that accompanies the slow leak of life from a body.

I have been seeing, lately, a man who is dying of non-Hodgkin's lymphoma. NHL is a disease of both the young and the old, like the benign comedy of Bill Cosby. A girl I knew in high school had NHL; she got all puffy from the treatment and then she was okay, she came back to school. But Chad is different; he has aggressive large-cell something or other. Aggressive: not Bill Cosby. He has the Sam Kinison of NHL. And nothing can shut it up. Not radiation. Not chemo, clinical trial after clinical trial until he maxed out. Now they're just trying to manage the pain.

Chad lives with his parents. When I come to the house, Chad's parents murmur quiet hellos and return to the kitchen to do crossword puzzles and watch daytime television. They know what I'm doing, but they also know their son is happier and calmer when I've visited. He needs less Oxycontin.

I knock on Chad's bedroom door and enter, not waiting for him to tell me to come in. I don't want him to expend any unnecessary energy.

He's lying in bed. The sheets are crisp blue and white, like an Oxford shirt. He's wearing soft cotton pajama bottoms and no top. Chad is good-looking, but pale. If he was ever puffy from his treatment, the puffiness is gone now. His hair has grown back, curly in the back. He's thin, but I've seen his high school senior portrait, and photos clipped from the local newspaper of his football glories are thumb-tacked to the wall above his desk. I know where the muscles used to be.

"Hey," I say softly. He grins.

I close the door.

I don't bother with how-are-you, or hand-holding, or any of that. That's not why I'm here. Besides, I know how he is. He's dying. I kick off my sneakers and slip out of my jeans, leaving them on the floor. I walk over to the bed, and straddle Chad on my knees. I begin unbuttoning my silk blouse, and his hands reach to help me. I push his hands gently back down to the bed.

"Save it," I whisper.

"Okay," he says, watching me.

My blouse is unbuttoned, and I run my hands over my bra. I lift my breasts slightly so that my nipples peek out over the tops of the cups. I touch my finger to Chad's mouth and he opens his lips, letting me wet my finger on his tongue. I circle my wet fingertip around my nipples, making them hard. I unhook the front clasp of my bra.

I slide my shirt and bra off together, so that I'm straddling Chad in just my panties. I lean forward so that my breasts hang over his face, my nipples grazing his lips. He takes one nipple in his mouth and sucks, and I moan. I'm not faking. I move so that he can switch to the other nipple, can even out my pleasure.

I start to kiss him, starting at his forehead, and then his cheeks, and then his mouth. Our tongues meet and I suck on his tongue, letting him know what else is in store. I continue moving my mouth down his body. His chest, now frail where barreling muscles used to be. His stomach, and the sinews that connect the stomach and hips and pelvis. I make a purring noise. This part of a man is always sexy to me.

Chad's dick is already half-hard. It never ceases to amaze me, the power of even a dying man's dick. I run the tip of my tongue from the base, near his balls, to the tip of the head. I taste the head in small licks. I slide my lips over his cock and work my way down. Chad groans and finds my breasts with his hands. He pinches my nipples and I groan with him. I slide my panties down and finger myself while I suck him.

Once I have Chad good and hard, and we are both slippery wet, I stop. I kick off my panties and rise up on my knees so that Chad can see my breasts again. I rub my clit against his dick, slowly, back and forth. I ease myself onto him, and he closes his eyes. There are pin-drop tears at the outer corners of his eyes.

"Open your eyes," I whisper. "Watch me." Chad is twenty-one. I know what he wants.

"I'm your own private porno flick," I whisper, and he grins at me. I love his grin. I cup my breasts in my hands and squeeze my nipples, I throw my head back so that my hair grazes my back. I rock back and forth, up and down on Chad's dick. I let go of my breasts and reach back with my hands to cup his balls. I think, it's a good thing the cancer has not metastasized to his testes. I think about how luck is relative.

He starts to moan, and I know he's ready to come. I lean forward so my chest is against his and nuzzle my mouth into his neck, hot breath and kisses and small whispers. I keep rocking.

He comes inside me. I know the results of his blood-work: he's clean. I don't need a condom. And I know I'm clear, and frankly, even if I wasn't, at this point it's irrel-evant to Chad anyway. I stay where I am, letting Chad ease out of my warmth when he's ready. I'm careful to support my weight with my thigh muscles, not to rest on his body.

I move so that I am lying next to Chad and pull the sheet over us. I rest my arm on his chest, the only time

I've put any weight on him.

"God, that felt great," I say.

Chad lets out a laugh. "To say the least," he says.

"I'm glad," I say.

"I wish I wasn't . . . you know," he begins.

"I know."

"No, I mean, I wish I wasn't dying so that I could keep doing this forever."

"But if you weren't dying, I wouldn't be here, sweetie. I'd be off fucking some other dying guy."

"Lucky me," Chad says.

"Yeah, well." Luck is relative. To say the least.

"I just wish," he says.

"Me too."

"This sucks."

"Yeah."

"Dying really sucks."

I hold his hand and put my face against his shoulder.

"I know it does," I say.

"I'm glad you don't say you're sorry. I am so sick of people saying to me, I'm sorry. Fuck that," he says. "I'm the one dying. I'm the one who's fucking sorry."

"Well, fuck sorry," I say, laughing.

"No, fuck me. Next week, right?"

"Yes," I say, "fuck you, next week."

"Cool," he says, closing his eyes. "Fuck dying."

My Email Man

Lori Lambert-Smith

In his messages, he addresses me as *belleza*
or preciosa. Sometimes he calls me
my sweet. He sends me poems

about Spanish Harlem, light
through a window and rain, words
that dip without warning into

second-person sex, images
that make me reach up
and slip the blouse off my shoulder.

My husband read one once.
He developed a keen and sudden interest
in poetry. He checks the email

frequently, knits his brows when he reads
my messages from Felipé. He says
he's afraid I'll leave him one day

for my online bard. I tell him *Don't be silly.*
He's married with three young sons. I'm married
with four children, in case you thought I forgot.

But I'm beginning to wonder
if my husband is right to be concerned.
Last night I dreamt I was making love to

Jose Feliciano. He called me *belleza, preciosa,
my sweet*. I woke up smiling. All day
I catch myself singing *Feliz Navidad.*

Bacon, Lola & Tomato

Susannah Indigo

The first time Lola found out that Keith had cheated on her, she gained ten pounds almost overnight. *I love you and I will wait for you, my sweet tomato*, his email note had said when she "accidentally" read it on his computer, which was cute, except that he certainly never referred to *her* as any kind of fruit or vegetable. "It's nobody," he offered with a guilty shrug as she sat slurping her second bowl of ramen noodles, "just a way to waste time online and avoid working on my novel."

"I am not a tomato," Lola Maria Estonia pointed out to him, just in case he had forgotten. She flipped her long black hair in the way that made men crazy and wrapped it around his wrists as though she could hold him that way. "But you do always wait for me."

They laughed; she forgave him; they made love; she got up afterwards while he slept and made herself a big bowl of Apple Jacks with raisins and four teaspoons of sugar.

The day Lola found his cell phone bill she discovered the joy of a box of Krispy Kremes, fresh and warm off the rack, half of them eaten directly while she was still in the bakery, the rest of the dozen melting in her mouth on the drive home. It appeared that the *sweet tomato* lived just one area code away and received almost daily calls ranging from ten minutes to two hours.

"I love you, Lola Maria," Keith swore that night when they crawled into their four-poster bed, the same bed they had shared for one year, two months, and twenty-three days. *"You are the heart of my dream,"* he whispered as he slid inside of her and gave the extra soft flesh on her bottom a spank. *"You are the voluptuous overflowing lush root of every desire any man has ever had."*

This was why she had moved in with him in the first place, because he had the words that could change the way she breathed. But now his words seemed to be adapting to her new body—he used to only call her *my fragile princess, my little girl.*

"I'm sorry I've hurt you," he whispered as they laid in bed with their legs entangled. "Is there anything I can do to make it up to you?"

She hated to think of fighting with him, or worse, to hear him lie again. "I'm *hungry,*" she finally answered, sure that more carbohydrates would make her vision of telephone bills disappear into sated bliss. So Keith got up and made her his special omelet with sausage and potatoes, no tomatoes, and for once she ate every single bite on her plate.

Lola Maria Estonia was up to a size 14 from her former size 8 when she finally went to visit the mysterious *tomato.* The sun was growing hotter and hotter as she stood on the sidewalk across the street from the address she had tracked down from the phone number. Lola was so fascinated that she took up more space in the world than she used to, even in the middle of the sidewalk, that she only smiled as the warmth grew under her red leather jacket, newly purchased from the Coldwell Collection in a comfy size for the "plus" woman. She had thrown out all of her old skinny jeans, although Keith had suggested that perhaps she should keep them because she would need them again soon. Lola had just smiled and gone shopping.

It didn't seem that Keith spent much face-to-face time with the *tomato*, because he was usually at home at his computer, or at his part-time job at the bookstore, or out with Lola. She wasn't about to ask Keith any more questions—she just monitored his email and phone calls, as though she was a detective. She also checked up on his novel that he said he was almost done with, and realized he hadn't written much of anything in a long time. *Why is it that I live with this man?* she wondered on her bad days, but then she remembered all the words, and how he made love to her with such passion, and how she was *almost* sure he was her soulmate, not to mention a good cook.

The *tomato* came out the front door of her small house and walked directly toward a Lincoln Town Car that was parked just beyond Lola. "Nice jacket," she said to Lola as she passed by.

"Would you like to have it?" Lola asked in an awkward gesture of friendliness that she hoped covered her desperation to find out more about this *tomato*. She had heard that people did this in some other places—Japan, maybe?—and suddenly it seemed like offering another woman her red leather jacket on a hot summer day was a normal thing to do.

The *tomato* stopped, turned, and laughed, taking Lola in fully from head to toe for the first time. Lola wore a long black cotton skirt, a white shirt with her black lace bra peeking out, and heavy silver jewelry. "Would I like it?" The tomato moved closer and stroked Lola's arm, checking the fabric, checking Lola, deciding. "Sure. It looks like a good fit."

"Thank you," whispered Lola in her smallest voice, though she knew she was the one who was supposed to say, "you're welcome." But she could not keep her eyes off the *tomato*—she had long curly red hair down to her waist, large breasts, great cleavage in a tight black tank top, and black jeans that looked to Lola like they were just about a size 14, maybe even 16. She was almost, Lola realized, identical in body to Lola's new look, and if Lola dyed her black hair red, she thought she could almost be her twin.

"My friends call me Cherry," said the *tomato,* slipping on the red jacket. "And you are . . .?"

"Lola Maria Estonia. Can I come with you?" Odd words were flowing out of her mouth, like someone else was writing them—better dialogue, she thought with a sharp twist of spite, than anything she had ever read in Keith's agonized attempts at novel writing.

"Do you know where I'm going?"

Lola couldn't guess, but she knew she wanted to be there. The curves on the *tomato's* hips were hypnotizing her, and she thought that maybe she wanted to touch them.

"To meet a man?" she guessed timidly. "My boyfriend's in love with you—maybe it's him?"

Cherry tomato laughed again, a long rollicking laugh, a laugh that Lola wanted to climb inside of and ride on, knowing it would carry her to a new place. "They're all in love with me, sweetheart," Cherry finally said. "Let's go eat meat."

The steakhouse was wood-paneled with high leather booths, an old-style male bonding place, complete with a private cigar room. Cherry tucked Lola into the booth seat and then slid in beside her. They each ordered the 14 ounce prime rib, baked potatoes with sour cream and butter, no salads, and chocolate amaretto pie for dessert.

"It's just phone-sex for me, sweetheart," Cherry explained between bites. "But as soon as I tell them I have long red hair and big tits, they're in love. The attention is great, along with the money. It supports my other passion."

"Keith has phone sex with you? Keith . . . pays . . . for phone sex??" Lola repeated in amazement.

"Keith? I don't remember their real names very well—what's he like?"

"Well, he's really smart . . . and he talks a lot, but I guess everyone must to have phone sex. His words—they're fancy, poetic, sometimes a bit over-the-top—he's a writer."

Cherry scooped up the last bite of pie and turned to feed it to Lola. "Open wide, sweetheart." As it melted in Lola's mouth, Cherry began to kiss her and lick her lips clean. "Yes, I know which one he is, baby," she whispered through the kisses. "I call him 'Bacon'—I give them all meat names, my little joke, but they think it's a macho compliment—he's a bit . . . greasy, isn't he, doesn't seem like your type."

Lola couldn't imagine why she should care, and could barely remember who he was herself. This woman, this *tomato,* this lovely plump mirror image of herself, was driving her wild with her lips and her fingers running up and down her legs. *Maybe this is why I just keep eating so much,* she thought, *to be worthy of someone like her.*

Cherry's fingers were high up her thigh under her skirt, beginning to stroke rhythmically toward her clit, when the waiter reappeared with the check. "Thanks," Cherry said to him, "we do have to hurry, we have someplace to be."

Lola assumed it would be her bed, or the backseat of the car, or anyplace nearby where they could continue. "No, sweetheart, I'm an organizer," the *tomato* explained to her on the way out. "We have a demonstration this afternoon. Consider yourself recruited—I promise you'll think of yourself differently after the day is done."

A group of about twelve women had gathered in the park just off of the Walnut Street open-air mall. They were holding signs, and there were hundreds of other people on the mall, most of them barely paying attention to the women. A few of the women were on rollerblades, one was doing tricks on her skateboard, and another had a baby on her hip.

Cherry parked the car and turned to Lola.

"They're waiting for me . . . for us, to start, baby. Take your shirt off."

"What?"

"Your shirt—take it off. Here, I'll help."

Lola decided this was a game, a tease, so she let Cherry unbutton her shirt and slip it from her shoulders.

"Nice, baby, good girl . . ." Cherry was unhooking Lola's bra and kissing her nipples, sucking on them, pulling slow and hard, sending the tingle right down to Lola's toes. "We should get them pierced," Cherry told her between kisses. "That always stops the cops."

"Cops?" Lola pulled away, just as two women with their picket signs approached the car and banged on the window for Cherry. The sign that Lola could see said: **TOPFREE! TAKE YOUR SHIRTS OFF FOR EQUALITY!**

"Yeah, you know, cops—pigs—that other mostly white meat around here," the *tomato* answered. "Technically, they can arrest us, but they rarely do, as long as we get the girls with the best tits to talk to them."

Cherry pulled Lola out of the car before she could answer, looping Lola's shirt into her jeans belt beside her own top she had stripped off. "You're a goddess," Cherry said as they joined the group on the lawn, "and you have as much right to be shirtless as any man does."

It *was* hot, and there *were* lots of men on the mall with their shirts off, and nobody looked twice at *them*. Lola watched as all the women around her took their tops off, in awe at the variety of breasts and backs and skin tones.

"They're beautiful," she whispered to the *tomato*.

"Exactly. So why is it that women have to keep their shirts on? Because they can feed babies from their nipples, a purely natural act? Or is it because women are nothing but sex objects to men, almost like pieces of . . . *meat*?"

Lola laughed and stood up a little prouder, her newly plump breasts perking up a bit more. "I've never even thought about it," she confessed.

"I know. Yet if you go out and do it by yourself somewhere, even on a beach, it's a criminal act. Equality for women is my passion, sweetheart, and nothing makes a stronger statement than this."

Lola had to agree as they began their march down the mall. Some people cheered, some booed, and a lot of men hooted and cat-called at them. But no one stopped them—Cherry went in the record shop to buy a CD, and though the manager asked her to put her shirt back on, she said "no," pointed to a man in the jazz aisle with his shirt off, and then proceeded to make her purchase and leave.

"*No.* That's about my favorite word for women." Cherry had big, gorgeous, heavy breasts, and though Lola was trying to think about politics and women's rights, sex was churning between her thighs. "No whining, no fuss, just *'no, I won't'* does wonders."

Lola trailed behind her like a puppy dog, trying to remember if she'd ever said "no" very firmly to Keith or any other man anywhere in her life.

"Hey, T-Bone, what's happening," the *tomato* said to a tall dark-haired man who greeted her near the central water fountain. Lola watched as the man kissed Cherry's hand, never touching her breasts, chatted for a few minutes, and then turned to go into a pizza shop.

"One of my clients," Cherry explained.

"Your *client?* They come here to see you? Does Keith . . . come . . . see you?" Lola raced over her words as she tried to wrap her mind around the sudden image of Keith seeing her half-naked in a public street mall.

"Bacon? He has. Some do—after I know them for a while, I tell them to stop by one of our demonstrations, it's good for them—seeing me in the flesh raises their consciousness and their cocks at the same time."

Lola stood speechless as she watched a security guard approach the group. He looked them all up and down—one woman was quietly breastfeeding while sitting on the edge of the fountain, others were chatting, some had packages from their purchases, and one woman with lovely brown breasts who looked like she might be sixty or so had pulled some yarn from her fanny-pack and was happily knitting and purling while waiting for the group.

"What do you think you're doing?" the guard said, a bit tentatively.

Cherry held Lola's hand. "Well, *she's* shopping for some new clothes, *Afton* there is making her granddaughter a sweater, and the *rest of us* are just relaxing." Cherry's breasts were about two inches from the guard's chest while she was talking, and Lola knew, just knew, that when he put his hands in his pockets it was not to pull out a gun, or even a ticket, but to keep himself from stroking her nipples. "Well . . . I think you should all put your tops back on, ma'am . . ."

"*No*. We can't do that. I know you believe that women and men are equal, right? So if you ask us to do that, you'd have to ask Bratwurst over there to do the same." She nodded toward a stocky brown-skinned man who had his shirt off and was talking with the woman on a skateboard. The guard looked toward him for an explanation.

Bratwurst just shrugged toward Cherry. "She's a *hot tomato*," he said with a wink at the guard.

"Yeah," echoed T-Bone, overhearing as he rejoined the group, pizza in hand. "And she's explained it clearly enough to *me*. Tits just want to be free."

"Well done, meat," Cherry whispered to the giggling Lola. "I train them well." The security guard rolled his eyes and shook his head. "Okay, *girls,* just be gone when I come back this way later."

"*No,*" the tomato said loudly to his departing back, but he didn't turn back to argue with her.

Lola never saw him again during the afternoon, though she imagined him hiding in shops and peeping at them whenever he could. After the rest of the group left for the day, Cherry dragged Lola into the Dress Barn Woman store, saying only, "Let's go change clothes."

In the dressing room, which fortunately had a wooden door that locked and went almost down to the floor, the *tomato* told Lola to strip.

"Everything?"

"Everything. Now. We're going to change clothes—with each other."

Lola pulled off her skirt and her panties and watched

Cherry take off her jeans. They stood side by side in front of the mirror and looked at each other, their breasts tanned from the afternoon of sun, their sturdy hips, their matching curves, their long hair only an inch or so different in length—*maybe not twins*, Lola thought, *but definitely sisters*.

Cherry held Lola in front of her and caressed her. "Watch me," she whispered as her hands ran down over Lola's belly and her fingers began to slide inside Lola, who was already soaking wet.

"Watch me watching you," Cherry whispered again, and Lola met her eyes as Cherry's thumb stroked her clit and two fingers twisted deep inside of her. "More," Lola sighed, "more. . . . more." Cherry slid a third finger inside of her as Lola leaned back against her and began to shudder.

"Open your eyes and watch," Cherry said, and she did, and all she could see was feminine skin and beauty and softness and her own trembling legs and Cherry's strong fingers bringing her to the finest orgasm she could ever remember having.

Cherry began to dress her in her jeans and tank top, but Lola protested that it was her turn. "Not yet, sweetheart," the tomato laughed. "Right now, I'm hungry."

"For what?"

"Bacon."

"I don't know if he'll be there," Lola said nervously as Cherry drove her home. "It doesn't matter," Cherry said with a smile, Lola's thigh pressed up against hers as she drove, her right arm draped around Lola's shoulder. "He'll come."

Lola thought maybe she wanted to stay sitting just as they were in Cherry's old-style car forever, with Cherry wearing Lola's skirt and shirt, minus the black lace bra since it wasn't quite big enough. They could drive around town, calling out new meat names for men, calling out to women to *take their tops off for equality!*, then ride off into the sunset, stopping every now and then to climb in the big back seat and fuck each other into some kind of happiness.

"Check the missed calls on my cell phone, baby, I'm sure you'll find he's around. But tell me, Lola, do you own a strap-on?"

Lola saw Keith's cell phone number on the phone, and tried to care, but she was too busy giggling at the idea of herself with a strap-on. "No, just a regular plug-in vibrator. We've never been too big on sex toys."

Cherry patted her shoulder like a child. "You'll find that Bacon has plenty."

"He does?"

"Yes, baby, check his gym bag that he never goes to the gym with."

The sudden curiosity growing over Lola was stronger than the rays of final evening sunlight piercing through their windows. "What do you do with him, Cherry? Why does he call you?"

"About the same as all meat, baby. They stroke themselves, they fantasize, I fantasize for them, they imagine sucking my tits . . ." she said, guiding Lola's head to that spot, unbuttoning one more button for her to imitate. "Then I almost always have them picture me with my big black strap-on fucking them up the ass, while they do it to themselves with their own dildoes and plugs."

Lola sucked, pressing her head hard to Cherry's breasts, while she felt her wetness almost flow down to her toes at Cherry's words.

"Yeah, I know," Cherry whispered softly to her, "it's hot, isn't it, baby. You can see why I do it for a living."

"He's never asked me for that," Lola said, coming up for air. "My finger there, maybe sometimes, but nothing else."

"And that's your answer, isn't it, why meat comes to the *tomato*—to get what they're not comfortable going for elsewhere. Don't worry, baby, we're here, and Bacon's got everything we need. We'll sizzle."

They took their tops off, even though it was dark, and ran up the stairs to Lola and Keith's place, but found no Bacon in sight. Lola found the gym bag immediately, and couldn't help but laugh at the variety found there.

"Let's greet him with them," Cherry said, starting to lay out a trail of toys from the front door to the bed with Lola's help. "Save these two, baby, that's what you'll need."

They raided the fridge and fed each other in bed; they raided each other and ate, and ate, until the entire apartment smelled like sex, and contentment. The sound of his key in the lock woke them both from their drowsy sexed-out sleep. Cherry jumped out of bed and covered Lola up with the quilt.

"You can't be here!" Keith said as the *tomato* stood in front of him stark naked and greeted him with a kiss. But she felt for his crotch and he was already hard, so she only laughed and walked him carefully through the toy-trail toward the bed.

"Lola will come home!" he tried again, but she assured him that wasn't a problem, and he began to lose track of his concern as she unbuttoned his shirt and kissed him again, hard. When he started moaning, she stopped undressing him, stepped back and said, "Bacon, strip."

He stripped for her, quickly. Lola popped up from

beneath the covers and stared. *Bacon.* Keith was tall and lean, and if Lola squinted at him just right he *did* look like a piece of bacon—hot, a little slippery, not necessarily good for you, but tasty.

"Lola!" He looked more than stunned, staring at the two voluptuous naked women in front of him, rather like he was watching both his wildest fantasy and his worst nightmare come true.

"Lola, get dressed," he said in his firmest boyfriend voice, trying to regain some control over the situation.

"*No,*" she said, and it sounded like someone else's voice, a strong voice, a voice that could stand up for itself anywhere in the world. "*No, I won't.*"

"Don't sweat, Bacon," the tomato jumped in. "We'll fuck *you,* you'll cook for *us,* we'll talk—*grill you* even maybe. It will all become clear."

Keith smiled, then frowned, but Lola noticed that his cock never went down. "Lola, I barely know this woman . . . nothing she's told you is true . . . you both need to get dressed, and she has to leave."

"*No,*" Lola said, this time in the voice of a goddess, a voice that owned not just its sexuality but its freedom, its joy, and the strength of a dozen proud women. She brought out the lube and his silver rocket dildo and held them up to him with a sweet smile. "*No. No more lies.*" She moved toward him and spanked his ass lightly. "Bend over, Bacon."

Contributors

Kim Addonizio (http://addonizio.home.mindspring.com) has authored several award-winning poetry books. Her story is taken from her collection of the same title, available from FC2. Recently she co-edited an anthology, *Dorothy Parker's Elbow: Tattoos on Writers, Writers on Tattoos* (Warner Books).

Arlene Ang lives in Venice, Italy, where she works as a freelance translator and Web designer. She is also the editor of the *Italian Niederngasse* (www.niederngasse.com). Her poetry has appeared in *sidereality, Poet's Canvas, Eclectica, Tryst* and *three candles*. She was the featured writer in the May 2003 issue of *Epiphany Magazine*.

Debbie Ann lives in a queer-poly-perverted household in San Francisco. Her work has also appeared in *Awakening the Virgin* and *Sex Toy Tales*.

Dorothy Bates is a former magazine editor/writer, lyricist, and writer of special material for cabaret performers. Her poetry has been published many times in print and on the Internet. Her work has also been published in the anthologies *Off the Cuffs* (Soft Skull Press) and *The Pagan Muse* (Kensington Publishing).

Jeff Beresford-Howe is a writer living in Oakland. He is a Contributing Editor at *Clean Sheets*, and writes a baseball column for *Slow Trains Literary Journal*.

Kell Brannon lives and writes near Chicago. In her spare time, she reads everything she can get her hands on, chases her wonderful partner around the house, and looks for interesting bugs in the woods.

Chris Bridges is the proprietor of *HootIsland.com*, a site devoted to silly sex in all its forms. Toward that end he has changed his natural inclination towards grim and tragic erotica and forced himself to create silly smut. Chris is married to an equally-silly wife and has two even stranger kids. He recently published a collection of funny erotica, *Giggling Into the Pillow*, and he writes a monthly column for erotica-readers.com, The Proud Humorsexual.

Rachel Kramer Bussel (www.rachelkramerbussel.com) is a freelance writer focusing on sexuality and popular culture. She is the reviser of *The Lesbian Sex Book*, co-author of *The Erotic Writer's Market Guide,* editor of *Horny? New York*, and co-editor of *Up All Night*, an erotica anthology. She is also a Contributing Editor at *Clean Sheets*. Her writing has been published in numerous magazines and newspapers including *Bust, Curve, Diva, Girlfriends, Playgirl, On Our Backs* and *The San Francisco Chronicle*, as well as in over a dozen erotic anthologies.

Diana Cage is the managing editor of *On Our Backs* magazine and the editor of the forthcoming anthologies: *The On Our Backs Guide to Sex*, and *Bottoms Up: A Collection of Punk-ass Porn*. She loves dirty words, naked ladies, motorcycles, and butch dykes who have a firm paddling hand.

M. Christian's (www.mchristian.com) work can be seen in *Best American Erotica, Best Gay Erotica, Best Lesbian Erotica, Best Transgendered Erotica, Best Bondage Erotica, Friction,* and over 150 other anthologies, magazines and Web sites. He's the editor of more than twelve anthologies, including *Best S/M Erotica, Love Under Foot* (with Greg Wharton), *Bad Boys* (with Paul Willis), *The Burning Pen, Guilty Pleasures,* and many others. He's the author of three collections, the Lambda-nominated *Dirty Words* (gay erotica), *Speaking Parts* (lesbian erotica), and *The Bachelor Machine* (science fiction erotica).

Isabelle Carruthers lives and writes in New Orleans, Louisiana. Formerly with the fiction staff of *Clean Sheets,* she is now on indefinite hiatus and devotes her time to a new marriage, extra kids, and restoring a decadent, decaying New Orleans bungalow. Her work has previously appeared in print in *Best Women's Erotica, The Mammoth Anthology of Best New Erotica, Prometheus, Slow Trains Literary Journal,* and *Spicy,* published by Mondadori (Italy), and in varied Web publications.

Ceridwen is a nomadic Celt, presently living in China, who loves poetry, music, dance, books and travel. Like her mythological namesake, the Welsh goddess of death and rebirth, she is concerned with the darker as well as the brighter aspect of life and love. Also a shapeshifter, she believes in the periodic transformation of her life. Her poetry has appeared online in *Clean Sheets, Erosha* and under her "own" name in *Litspeak Dresden.*

Naomi Darvell is an Articles Editor for Clean Sheets.

William Dean is Associate Editor for *Clean Sheets Magazine.* He also writes a monthly column, "Into the Erotik" for the Erotica Readers & Writers Association. His works have appeared in Marilyn Jaye Lewis' *Other Rooms, Mind Caviar, Literotica, Slow Trains, SoHo Literary Journal, Night Charm*, and other online sites. His stories have also appeared in the anthologies: *From Porn to Poetry 1, Tears on Black Roses*, and *Love Under Foot.* He lives in Southern California.

Adrianna de la Rosa is the nom de plume of an artist and writer who lives in a southern California beach town. She loves: traveling, sarongs, balmy places, tiramisu, champagne cocktails, all kinds of gardens, hats, and most of all—the sublime and beautiful erotic poetry of Octavio Paz. Her work has appeared in *Clean Sheets* and *Slow Trains Literary Journal.*

Jane Duvall has been trying to prove for years that it is possible to have seemingly contradictory parts. Mother of three, narrator of her own intimate personal history, sometimes writer and model, hobbyist photographer, homebody with a healthy interest in gourmet cooking and canning, and a burgeoning career in the arena of physical fitness and wellbeing are just a few of her roles and interests so far. You can find her online at *www.janesguide.com* and *www.janeduvall.com.*

Robert Fawn is a poet, playwright, and surrealist. His plays have been performed throughout the United States and in Europe. He is presently working on *The Autobiography of Robert Fawn*, which will be a surrealist book of memoirs documenting his reality as a transvestite.

Diane Fisher is a freelance writer and graduate student living in Boulder, Colorado.

Shanna Germain (www.shannagermain.com) is an author, photographer, soy mocha drinker, racquetball player, and nudist-for-peace in Portland, Oregon. She is also the Editor-in-Chief of *Nervy Girl* magazine, and the Managing Editor of both her husband and her cat.

Robert Gibbons recently resigned his position from an academic library in Boston to pursue his writing career full time. His first full-length book, *Slow Trains & Beyond: Selected Work* is forthcoming from Samba Mountain Press.

Maggie Gray is a writer of poetry, fiction, and nonfiction living in Pennsylvania. Her writing has appeared recently in *Clean Sheets* and *The Experimental Forest*. Her work is scheduled to appear in The Philadelphia Writer's Conference 2003 anthology and in *Mothering* magazine.

Aprill Hewitt (eroticollage@hotmail.com) has lived as a gypsy in several countries, studied feminism and BDSM, finally moving to New York City to live as a bohemian writer/poet/erotic art therapist. She now travels across the country giving workshops called "Eroticollage—Exploring Your Sexuality Through The Arts", promoting her CD, *Erotic Whispers, Scandolous Spoken Word,* and her upcoming book, *Eroticollage.* See more of her work at her Web site on www.blackplanet.com. under "Eroticollage".

Susannah Indigo (www.susannahindigo.com) is the editor-in-chief of Clean Sheets (www.cleansheets.com), and also the editor and founder of Slow Trains Literary Journal (www.slowtrains.com). She is the author of *Oysters Among Us* and *Many Kisses: Stories of Dominant Love*, and the co-editor of the *From Porn to Poetry* series. She lives in Denver, Colorado.

Joy James (joyce.james@att.net) is a writer based outside Washington, D.C. Her erotica has appeared frequently in *Clean Sheets*, as well as other Web sites. Two of her recent stories have been included in the print anthologies *Best Fetish Erotica* and *Erotic Travel Tales*.

Rebecca Lu Kiernan has published in *Ms Magazine*, *Asimov's Science Fiction, Space and Time*, and other publications in the U.S. and Australia. Her new book, *The Man Who Remembered Too Much*, is currently available to media only. She has been nominated for a Rhysling Award.

Mike Kimera is fascinated by the way sex and lust shape peoples' lives. His stories, which range from the tender and intimate to the dark and dangerous, have been featured in *From Porn to Poetry 1, Desires,* and *Sacred Exchange*. He works as a management consultant and lives in Switzerland.

Lori Lambert-Smith's poetry has appeared in many print publications, including *Atlanta Review* and *Proposing on the Brooklyn Bridge—Poems About Marriage*, and online at *PoetryMagazine.com* and *CleanSheets.com*. She lives in Richland, Washington.

Dorianne Laux is the author of three collections of poetry from BOA Editions, *Awake* (1990), introduced by Philip Levine, *What We Carry* (1994), finalist for the National Book Critics Circle Award, and *Smoke* (2000). She is also co-author, with Kim Addonizio, of *The Poet's Companion: A Guide to the Pleasures of Writing Poetry* (W.W. Norton, 1997).

Gary Meyer is a freelance editor, part-time critic, and full-time hedonist. Retired from an information systems career, he collects transgressive literature and supports his wife as cook, butler, and head cat wrangler. When not doctoring prose or mincing garlic, he's likely to be found at the local art cinema or hiking in the high desert.

Bill Noble is a nationally-recognized poet and short story writer who had every intention of living out his sunset years as the protagonist of his very own Proustian, Miller-esque erotic tale. When he's not pecking away at a keyboard, trying to salvage his literary reputation, he's a fiction editor at *Clean Sheets* . . . where he pecks away at a keyboard.

Performance poet **Jennie Orvino's** CD, *Make Love Not War* (www.soundofpoetry.com), explores the body erotic and the body politic in collaboration with some of San Francisco's most accomplished musicians. She produces "Poetic License" for community radio KRCB-FM 91 in Sonoma County, California. Publication credits include *slowtrains.com, cleansheets.com, poetsagainstwar.org.uk,* Good Vibrations' *Sex Toy Tales, The Dickens,* and *New York Quarterly*.

Brian Peters is the managing editor for *Clean Sheets*, and an assistant editor for *Slow Trains Literary Journal*.

Julia Peters is a nice girl from Brooklyn. Her first published story in *Clean Sheets,* "Troy", began a long and happy road to her current position as a fiction editor. Julia's work has appeared under various names in *Playgirl, Mind Caviar, Thermoerotic* and others. The rest of her time is spent walking her dog, running her own business, hitting the snooze button, howling at the moon, and finding inspiration for the next story.

Alex M. Quinlan lives on the East Coast of the United States, with two cats, two children, and two spouses. You can see more of her work in *Prometheus (*www.tes.org) and *Consent (*www.consentmag.com).

Gary Sandman is a writer and painter living in New York City. He has written *Ceremonies* and *Resistance,* both novels, as well as *Quaker Artists*, an art history. He has published in *Friends Journal.* His recent drawings have been line sketches in ink. All he has ever wanted to do is to write and paint and live in Paris.

Lawrence Schimel has published over 60 books, including *His Tongue; Switch Hitters: Lesbians Write Gay Male Erotica and Gay Men Write Lesbian Erotica; PoMoSexuals; The Drag Queen of Elfland;* and *Kosher Meat.* He's won the Lambda Literary Award and the Rhysling Award, among other prizes. His writings have been published in Basque, Catalan, Czech, Dutch, Esperanto, Finnish, French, Galician, German, Hungarian, Italian, Japanese, Polish, Portuguese, Romanian, Russian, Slovak, Spanish, and Swedish translations. He currently lives in Madrid, Spain.

Heather Shaw (http://users.lanminds.com/gryffyn) is the author of short fiction, poetry, and articles on everything from sex to San Francisco. Her work has appeared in *Strange Horizons, Slow Trains,* and the anthology *Skin Deep*. She lives in Oakland with her fiance, sister, and 5-month-old nephew.

Marcy Sheiner is the editor of *Herotica 4, 5, and 6,* as well as of the annual *Best Women's Erotica* series. All her books, including *Sex for the Clueless: How to Have a More Erotic and Fulfilling Life,* and *Perfectly Normal: A Mother's Memoir* are available on Amazon.com or via her Web site (http://marcysheiner.tripod.com/).

Nola Summers lives and writes in Toronto, Ontario. She is a Contributing Editor for *Clean Sheets* and is studying to be an astrologer. One day she hopes to combine the astral aspects of life with the erotic. She has been published in *Clean Sheets, Slow Trains*, and *The Mammoth Book of Best New Erotica* (2002).

Jim Tolan lives in Staten Island, New York, and has had poems in such places as *American Literary Review, Atlanta Review, Bellevue Literary Review, Indiana Review, Luna*, and *Many Mountains Moving*. His manuscript, *She Built a Church. He Raised the Steeple*, co-authored with Aimee Record, is in circulation.

Marnie Webb (http://www.crankreport.org) lives and writes in the San Francisco Bay Area. She has been published in various online and print publications and is currently working on a collection of short fiction.

Greg Wharton is the publisher of Suspect Thoughts Press, and an editor for two Web magazines, *SuspectThoughts.com* and *VelvetMafia.com*. He is the author of the collection *Johnny Was*, and editor of the anthologies *The Best of the Best Meat Erotica, Law of Desire* (with Ian Philips), *The Love That Dare Not Speak Its Name, Love Under Foot* (with M. Christian), and *Of the Flesh*. He lives in San Francisco with his honey Ian Philips.

Aria Williamson is a teacher and poet. Her work has been published in many print and online journals, including *Clean Sheets* and *From Porn to Poetry 1*.

Emanuel Xavier, once a prostitute from New York City's West Side Highway piers, is said to be one of the most significant voices to emerge from the neo-Nuyorican poetry movement. His books include the novel, *Christ-Like,* and the poetry collections, *Pier Queen* and *Americano*. He is a recipient of the Marsha A. Gomez Cultural Heritage Award for his contributions to gay and Latino culture.

ORDER FORM

SAMBA MOUNTAIN PRESS
P.O. BOX 4741
ENGLEWOOD, CO 80155
www.sambamountain.com
Email: info@sambamountain.com

TITLE	QTY	PRICE
From Porn to Poetry 1 *(2001)*	_____	$ 16.00
From Porn to Poetry 2 *(2003)*	_____	$ 16.00
Oysters Among Us: *Erotic Tales of Wonder*	_____	$ 14.95
Blue: The Color of Desire *by Patrick Linney*	_____	$ 12.00
Many Kisses: *Stories of Dominant Love*	_____	$ 13.00
Blow Jobs & Lemon Kisses: *The Clean Sheets Cookbook For Sex*	_____	$ 8.95

*shipping via Media Mail to
   the U.S. is included in pricing
*order by check via USPS, or
   credit card online only

Clean Sheets Magazine

Editor-In-Chief	Susannah Indigo
Managing Editor	Brian Peters
Associate Editor	William Dean
Articles Editors	Naomi Darvell, William Dean
Exotica Editors	Samantha Capps Emerson, Brian Peters
Fiction Editors	Bill Noble, Julia Peters
Poetry Editor	Devan Macduff
Reviews Editor	Shanna Germain
Newsletter Editor	/amqueue
Web Editors	Hipster Doofus, Sefinat Otaru
Contributing Editors	Jeff Beresford-Howe, Rachel Kramer Bussel, Gary Meyer, Ann Regentin, Nola Summers
Galley Slaves	Nola Summers, Jenn Wilson, Shirin Shoai, Teresa Newsome, maya

www.cleansheets.com